RED SKY

Ron Rendleman

Other Books By Ron Rendleman

Tears For A King
Disciple in Blue Suede Shoes
You Can't Fly Home Again
Fistful of Dust
Stepping Into The Supernatural

Red Sky

Copyright © 1996 by Ron Rendleman

Published by Sterling Productions
P.O. Box 41
Sterling, Illinois 61081

Printed in the United States of America

Library of Congress Catalog Card Number 96-67098

ISBN 0-9650884-0-5

Prologue

While Scott White's story may be fictional, the excerpts from radio interviews and books, and statements by militia leaders and other personages, are authentic. A list of those who indirectly contributed information is included at the end.

If a man does not keep pace with his

companions, perhaps it is because he hears

a different drummer. Let him step

to the music he hears, however measured

or far away.

Henry David Thoreau

Introduction

Many Americans believe that our country will soon be immersed in a civil war. Normally peaceful citizens will refuse to surrender their guns to a government seemingly intent on imposing the agenda of the New World Order. America the beautiful will become the land of sorrows.

It didn't have to happen but it was predictable. History records that when people refuse to bend their knee to their Creator, they fall victim to tyrants and often extinction at the hands of an enemy from without.

In days of old, most Americans lived by Christian principles in a spirit of thankfulness and humility. But then they began to take their blessings for granted, and became self-indulged and prideful and carelessly slumbered while dark forces went about their sinister work.

As the hour grew later, the only hope the country had were the people who knew God personally. That hope was found in 2 Chronicles 7:14 of the Bible. "If my people who are called by my name will humble themselves, pray, seek my face and turn from their wicked ways, then will I hear from Heaven, forgive their sin and heal their land."

But His people didn't believe Him, and to their already long list of sins they added still another called "religious spirit," where they did many things *for* God but none *with* Him.

Always faithful to warn His people before His judgment falls, God began speaking to America through His prophets. But the leaders of the country, and the pastors and teachers, ignored them and did not prepare the people.

In Luke 21:20 and 21, Jesus told His followers, "When you see Jerusalem surrounded with armies... flee." These words came back to the brethren three dozen years later when Jerusalem was surrounded by the Roman army. While over a million people were slaughtered and the survivors sold as slaves, the brethren who took the Prophet's warning seriously, escaped.

Proverbs 27:12 states: "The prudent see danger and take refuge, but the simple keep going and suffer for it."

I trust that Scott's story will prompt you to do additional research. Don't take anybody's word. Keep informed with the Internet, buy a short-wave radio, but don't be one of the "sheeple" who still believe the mainstream media is committed to telling the truth.

The day is coming when the "sheeple" will obediently report to a government office to be injected with their very own hi-tech, state-of-the-art, computer identity implant chip. You, hopefully, will head for the woods and cry out to your Maker — rather than accept the *mark of the beast*.

ONE

Scott White, former high school star athlete and college degree hopeful, but now a family man and dreamer of stale dreams, drove his cab down Chicago's Wells Street. He had skidded around on snowy streets all day, almost had two accidents, and now was glad to be checking in.

The antique shops he passed had already turned on their window lights. Ancient stained glass, brass bed frames, and polished silverware came alive. He thought of Amy.

Christmas was a week away and he was broke. Every dollar of his next paycheck had a place to go—he'd be lucky to squeeze out enough for a stuffed animal for his little boy.

Impulsively, Scott pulled the cab over to the curb. He saw it before he opened the shop's door—a magnificent silver candlestick, its patina polished to a pale blue satin. His thoughts jumped back to those beautiful nights when they were first married and he and Amy ate dinner by candlelight. Things were better, then, much better. But then the baby came and bills began, and several pieces of Amy's lifetime antique collection, including her candlesticks, were sacrificed.

The owner was closing the store. He gave Scott a quick once over, noticed his faded jeans, black leather

1

jacket and shoulder length hair, and continued covering the flatware.

"I'm interested in your candlestick. Victorian, isn't it?"

The shopkeeper kept working. "Early Victorian. Came in recently with some other things."

Scott examined it, noticing its rococo style with classic foliate border, the exact treatment he had seen on other sterling Amy admired so in shops she dragged him to. He found the maker's mark on the base.

"How much you asking?"

"Sixty-five."

Scott wasn't as knowledgeable as Amy, but he was sure it was worth more. A lot more. But there was no way he could manage sixty-five dollars. Sighing, he put it back. "I'm a little short right now. Maybe I'll stop in later."

"We take credit cards—Mastercharge, Visa..."

"I don't use them."

"You can fill out a credit application. We can have an answer in a couple of days."

Scott chewed his lower lip. He could just see Amy's expression when she opened the package. He almost said "Okay," but then shook his head. "No, thanks, maybe I'll work out something else."

Returning to his cab, he rested his forehead on the steering wheel. "God," he half sobbed, "when am I gonna be able to breathe? I'm sick of being broke."

Though he was late checking in, he walked home slowly through the softly falling snow. He trudged up three flights to the tiny two-room flat on Chicago's near north side and found the table set and Amy washing lettuce at the sink. Tall, and normally lithe and angular, she was carrying a lot more weight with this child, and Scott didn't like it. She turned and smiled.

"You're late. Was it hard driving?"

He pecked her on the cheek. "Hard enough."

They sat down to rice and soybeans for the fourth night in a row, and it was all he could do to keep from throwing them against the wall. But it wasn't her fault.

After supper Amy worked some on her needlepoint, waiting for their landlady to pick her up for her doctor's appointment.

She watched Scott get up and move around restlessly, finally pick up his guitar and tune it—the first time in months. He began to hum *Amazing Grace* very softly, and it brought tears to her eyes. How he used to sing and play, and to laugh! His carefully kept Gibson was not just a guitar—it was half his soul.

He had been growing increasingly moody and restless for some time now. She could only guess it was because there would soon be another mouth to feed.

The landlady arrived. Scott kept strumming even when Amy kissed him goodbye.

But he stopped when the door closed and stared at the floor for a long time. He put the guitar away and began to pace. He wished he didn't have to stay with the kid. He felt like going out somewhere, anywhere he could unwind.

He lit a cigarette, walked to the window, and listened for sound from the boy as he passed the bedroom door. It had stopped snowing. The "Drugs" sign flashed on and off at the corner, and he thought about the new cashier. She was built all right, but he felt guilty immediately and tried to put her out of his mind.

Old friends had told him he was nuts for getting married so young. "We'll give ya a year," they jeered. Yeah, but that first year was the berries. Everything went smooth, nice—they really had it.

Then David came and everything changed. Okay, all right, so the kid's cute. But hey, I'm still here, remember me? But never mind about that. Just push the hack till your eyes blur so you can pay the extra bills, come home with nerves shot, start yelling, and see the kid run and hide behind her. Hurts bad. The kid's scared of you.

He left the window and took a small model boat down from a shelf over the kitchen sink. He looked at it critically and set it on the table. It was when he was like this that it really helped, making the boats. He felt himself relax till all the noise of the jungle, all his troubles faded, and he was off again to the South Seas.

When the blade slipped, almost ruining the model, he stopped. Even this was no good. He went into the bedroom, flopped down on the bed, and switched on the short-wave receiver on the nightstand. It was a compact digital, not nearly as expensive as the ham rig he had sold to buy Amy's wedding ring, but it received well, even on an indoor wire strung up over the window. He began pushing the memory buttons for the patriot frequencies for the latest news on the militia, but the fading and static were bad. He switched it off and went back to the kitchen window.

For once, no one had left a newspaper in the cab and there was nothing in the flat he hadn't read. He looked every place and then he sat and tried to think about something else. He could run down to the corner for a paper. Yeah, if the boy was sleeping maybe it would be okay.

He opened the bedroom door a crack. The boy lay quiet, eyes closed, clutching a corner of his sheet. Scott tiptoed in and covered him with a blanket.

Looking down at his son, he thought of something Amy once said. "You've got to show feeling for him

4

before you can expect any in return." Yeah, maybe so, but how do you control a temper that's been honed to a fine edge from ten hours of grinding? He threw on a coat and left the apartment, fixing the lock on the outer door so it wouldn't snap.

It had gotten much colder. He filled his lungs and felt a little light-headed. The street was quiet and the new snow glowed fluorescently from a full moon.

At the drug store the girl was near the cash register, alone.

"Hi," he said. "Gimme' a *Trib*, huh?"

She turned for the paper, that profile perfect. He stared, he had to. "How's business?" he asked.

"Jumpin', can't you see?"

He laughed nervously, then said, "You're new, aren't you?"

"Yes," she smiled, twilight-lovely eyes locked on his. He looked away and pretended to study the front page of his paper.

"You from around here?" he asked a little hesitatingly.

"No," she answered. "Just moved here two weeks ago. I'm a stranger, don't know a soul." She told him she used to live with a girlfriend but they couldn't get along. She told him all about it, but he hardly listened. He fumbled with a cigarette, took another look at the paper, then said as calmly as he could, "What time you get off?"

"About ten."

He hesitated, then said, "Maybe, I'll drop by some night."

She smiled.

He fantasized about her the next day on the job. He thought of alibis that would get him out of the house at night.

At noon he stopped for a sandwich south of the Loop and noticed an old sightless black man outside the restaurant, strumming an ancient guitar and singing *Oh Holy Night*. The way he handled it made Scott stop. His hair was white and his clothes shabby, but he held his head high and Scott wondered how he could sing and make a guitar sound that good in the cold. He noticed the tin cup and the pamphlets in it, dropped in a quarter, and took one of the papers. It was a Christian tract. He waited for the song to end.

"Mighty fine," he said.

"Well, thank you kindly."

"How do you keep that old guitar sounding so good in this cold?"

"Oh, I dunno. I just speak to it nice and treat it nice and it just treats me nice."

"Can I buy you a cup of coffee?"

"You lead the way."

He led the old man inside to the counter and learned his name was Ezra. Scott didn't have enough for two sandwiches so he ordered two coffees and skipped lunch. He read Ezra's pamphlet about Christmas and as they sat talking quietly, mostly about the old man's life, Scott noticed he never once complained or had a bad word for the kids or derelicts who had robbed from him through the years. He called it an "occupational hazard."

"I hope you don't misunderstand, but I'd like to ask you something personal," Scott said.

"Speak your heart, son."

"Don't you ever get just a little uptight because you were made blind by a war started by politicians?"

The old man chuckled and adjusted his sunglasses. "No, son. It's true I can't see the sunset like you can. But when the clouds cover your sky, I keep seein' my

6

pretty sunsets just the same. My ears hear the little sounds yours may miss, and my hands touch the trees God put here for me. I color all my pictures just the way you'd probably want yours to be but no, son, I really don't mind being blind, for God is the next thing I'll see."

Scott spent the rest of the day in the cab reflecting on Ezra's words. If anyone deserved a medal for sticking out a crummy life, it had to be the old man. He lay awake for a long time that night, going over his life, trying to sort out his fears, his goals, his failures, and it became obvious he needed to make some changes, including treating his woman better.

He was up early and out of the house before Amy stirred. It was important that she didn't see him take the guitar. Though it was worth much more, the pawn shop dealer finally agreed on seventy dollars. He grabbed up the money and headed straight for the antique shop on Wells.

She cried on Christmas morning when she learned of his sacrifice. She rubbed the sterling candlestick lovingly. It didn't make the slightest difference, nor would she ever tell him, that when she carefully examined the maker's mark on the base and saw its freshness, she knew the candlestick was a fake.

TWO

Lady Spring had come at last, dancing through parks and ghettos, splashing a fragrance that, when whiffed, caused a strange type of fever. From Evanston to Calumet Park, a mad winter had succeeded in turning Chicago's lake shore into a frozen no man's land, but Spring just smiled her lovely smile, made a little gesture, and winter's madness had gone.

Scott pulled his cab into the line at the Sherman House, turned off the ignition, leaned his head out the open window, and let the warm sun caress him. His face was lean and angular with close-set eyes, large nose and strong jaw, and was wizened beyond his twenty-four years.

He was feeling better these days; it almost seemed like God was smiling down on him for a change. A baby girl had come whom he had wanted a lot. He wasn't losing his temper with the public nearly as much, he hadn't dented the cab lately, and even his tips were better.

Old Ezra still sang of life and pain and God, and Scott continued to be envious of the old man's secret to joyful survival. He had grown to love the old man, and had to admit he sought his approval. Perhaps, it was because his own dad had left his mom when he was very young and he never had the encouragement so necessary for self-confidence, that he was so drawn to Ezra. The black man was always building him up. Sometimes, Scott would throw his guitar, retrieved from the pawn shop, into the cab's trunk, and he and Ezra would jam a blues or country piece. Often, they drew decent crowds and Scott was glad for the old man's sake when his cup filled with bills.

One day in early April, he was driving down Rush street when a foxy well-built lady, complete with tight skirt and sweater, pranced in front of his cab at a stoplight. He would have kept staring except for the guilt that hit him; it was almost as though Ezra was sitting in the front seat with him.

He cut down on smoking, reduced his beer drinking, and even started reading the New Testament. Actually, he considered himself not that bad a Christian, compared to his drinking buddies. But compared to Ezra, that was another story. Sometimes he'd park his cab a half a block from the restaurant and just watch him. No matter how little money came his way, no matter how often the kids harassed him, Ezra just kept singing with all of his heart.

One day they were sitting in their usual booth at the restaurant when Scott blurted out, "Ezra, how did you find God?"

Ezra chuckled. "Find God? God's every which way. No matter where you turn, you bump into Him."

"Na, I'm serious."

"So am I."

"I think He plays hide and seek."

" Depends. "

"On what?"

"How bad a man wants to find Him. Most folks think they serious but most times they just want a ladder to git off the roof 'cause the house is on fire."

9

"You know, when I was a kid my ma made me go to Sunday school at a Baptist church. I think I wanted to know God then. I raised my hand with the other kids for Christ to come into my life but I don't know..."

"Whatcha mean, you don't know?"

"They said I was saved, but how do you know for sure?"

Ezra thought it over. "If you serious, He'll let you know where you are wid Him."

"You know what really bugs me?"

"I'm listenin'."

"My life. I go to work, come home, go to sleep, get up, go back to work, and for what? To pay bills. To bend my knee to the almighty god of commerce."

"What about that lovely family you always braggin' on?"

"I know, I know...but there's got to be more to life than workin' to eat and waitin' to die. Sometimes I get the feeling I need to do something really big, something the whole world will know about, something that would maybe even make God clap His hands."

Ezra was smiling. "Sounds like the makings of a dream. Go out and find it. Just remember, it can take you a long way off, let you do impossible things, or it can eat you up like cancer. But make no mistake, it's better to chase a dream than be guilty of the greatest sin of all, outside of ignorin' God Almighty, that is."

"What's that?"

"A wasted life. And right behind that is the sin of a wasted talent."

Scott stirred his coffee intently.

"You know what I'm driving at, don't you?"

Scott nodded.

"You got some real talent, son. You want to do something worthwhile, keep writing them songs that come from your heart. So what if you never make a name or the big buck. You'll have the satisfaction of knowin' you're a voice cryin' in the wilderness for those homeless folks livin' under the Wacker Street bridge, for the old folks our society has forgotten, for all those ghetto kids without dads."

"You sound like Martin Luther King."

"Maybe so, but he had a dream and he helped a lot of other folks dream, too."

"But it cost him."

"That it did. But if you dream big, sometimes you pay big."

Now, Scott sat in the cab line at the Sherman House drinking in the sun, wondering if all his good intentions would ever become hardly more than that. It would take more than wishful thinking to accomplish big things; it would take a lot of hard work and sacrifice. He had had a taste of that. He had become an amateur radio operator as a young teen by studying theory and code on his own one summer, instead of hitting the beach with his friends. He had heard a ham in Tahiti describe his island to a Puerto Rican ham on an old Halicrafter receiver he bought at a garage sale, and he became plagued with "RF" virus. That was the only summer he didn't work to help Ma pay the bills.

His next project was learning the guitar and this, too, he did without help. He paid for his Gibson acoustic by saving every extra dime over three years. Some who heard him thought he should have kept it up, but the songs he wrote and liked to sing best were what Ezra called "songs from the heart," like Woody Guthrie's songs of the oppressed, songs that one died broke doing.

Though he felt cheated that he had never gone to college, he knew his helping out took the burden off

Ma.

"Don't worry, Ma, I won't walk out on you like the old man did," he would tell her often to reassure her. He tried to be there always for her to lean on, especially when his younger brother, Mike, got out of line.

Until that day in September, a week after his nineteenth birthday, the day he would never forget. They were strolling through Lincoln Park when Amy made the announcement. Neither of them even considered an abortion or adoption, and though she gave him a choice, marrying her was the only thing to do. The thing that tore him up though, was the look of uncertainty and fear in Ma's eyes when he told her that he had to break his promise to her. But he checked in on her often, and Mike had graduated and was starting to bring home a good check, so they managed.

And if he felt trapped by his life he had only himself to blame. Yet, he was very lucky. Amy was everything he could want in a mate—level-headed, faithful, full of devotion, and very patient with his mood swings.

But what was it Ezra had said about a dream? He had desire without direction, willingness to sacrifice, but without a cause worthy. All he had for sure was something nagging at him, a constant restlessness that he was not doing what he should be. He had a growing desire to change his life style, to be more in control. He had changed a lot in six months, he could change more. He knew he could quit smoking and drinking completely, once he made up his mind.

The driver behind nudged his bumper; he wanted Scott to pull up. Scott waved and put the cab in motion. When he reached the head of the line, a well dressed man in his sixties got in.

"Board of Trade, driver, and don't spare the

horses!"

As Scott drove through the heavy noon traffic, he glanced occasionally at his passenger's anxious face in the mirror and an uneasy feeling touched him. That night as he lay in bed, the man's stressful face kept coming to him.

The next day he was driving past a religious bookstore when he impulsively pulled over and parked. He walked around the store aimlessly, discovered the tract rack, and bought a hundred pamphlets he figured Ezra would like.

But his very next passenger was a big man, foulmouthed, who noticed every woman they passed. *It's no big thing*, he told himself, *just give him one*. But suddenly the glass partition behind him had become a wall of concrete. The tracts lay beside him on the seat the rest of the day, a constant reminder of his cowardice.

That night he slept restlessly. The next day he awoke with a resolve that the very first person who got in his cab would get a tract. He was just pulling out of the garage when the night dispatcher coming off his shift, jumped in. Scott's heart began to race. The man was a cynic and prejudiced against religion. Looming large in his mind was a scene of being called into the superintendent's office and losing his job. He waited till the dispatcher got out, then thrust the tract through the window.

"Here George, check this out." he said.

George stood in the street and looked the pamphlet over carefully and finally put it in his pocket. When he stooped and peered through the window, something about his face had changed. "Thanks, I'll read it," he said quietly.

Scott could have stopped then, but for some reason

he kept passing the tracts to certain passengers; and he wondered if this burden he was feeling was a calling, an answer to his recent prayers in the middle of the night not to be guilty of the greatest sin of all—a wasted life.

One day he was driving down Clark St. and he had a crazy thought to park the cab and take some tracts into one of the taverns. The place he entered was a typical honky-tonk—dark, juke box blasting country music, the bar lined with both men and women, some very young. The bartender was in the rear frying hamburgers.

Scott started at the far end and put a pamphlet beside each elbow. He was half way up the bar when it grew quiet as the reason for his presence became known.

A heavy set man swung drunkenly around. "This about church?" he demanded.

"Not exactly...," Scott answered.

"We don't need this crap in here." The man crumpled the tract and threw it on the floor, "This ain't no church." Scott shrugged and kept moving.

Two seats further down, a petite blonde about thirty-five, with telltale lines around the mouth women who drink a lot get later in life, touched his arm as he passed. She was pretty far gone. "I'm Irene. You fool around, hon?"

"Pardon?"

"I said, do ya fool around?"

Scott cleared his throat. "No, Ma'am. I'm married."

"Too bad." She took a tract. "But I'll read your paper."

When he reached the last man he noticed the bartender coming up the bar fast, a frown on his face. Scott headed for the door, then turned, smiled at the bartender, and gave him a two finger salute.

"Were you scared, Scotty?" Amy asked at supper, her large brown eyes flashing wide.

"Yeah, I was scared. It was a real trip."

"You going to keep doing it?"

"Maybe. Maybe not. I don't even know why I did it." He thought about it. "But I'll tell you this. All you have to do is look into their eyes—there's nothing there, like dead people."

"I'll be praying for you," Amy said, softly. He knew she meant it. She didn't talk about it much, but he envied her never wavering conviction that God heard every prayer uttered.

Two days later, he was driving past a large office building under construction. Scores of hard-hatted workmen sat, shoulder to shoulder, on the sunny sidewalk with their backs against the building, eating their lunches and gawking at young secretaries hurrying past. Then Scott saw something that he didn't believe at first. Many of the men had gotten down very low on the sidewalk and were trying to look under the girls' dresses. Any condemnation he might have felt was quickly squelched by the raw knowledge that at one point in his life he might have tried the same trick himself.

The next day he was back at the bookstore. He bought 200 tracts entitled, *This Was Your Life*, a cartoon story of a man who drops dead drinking a martini in his back yard and is forced to look at a movie screen account of his life.

When the men came out at noon, Scott started down the line, giving a booklet to each one. When he finished, he was tempted to cross the street, the shortest way to his cab, but he deliberately went back past the men—past their stares and wisecracks. Toward the end of the line, two young guys about his age were laughing over the booklet. Scott squatted in front of them.

"You know, guys, *Playboy* magazine used to be my Bible," he said. "And I've raised a lot of hell. But the next morning I'd have to get up and start living with my guilty conscience again."

The younger guy's smirk slowly faded, and in his dark, good-looking eyes, Scott saw a very real hate reveal itself—for a moment it looked like the guy was getting ready to throw a punch. But instead, he jumped up and went back into the building with his friends.

For a long time Scott sat in his cab staring at the colossal tower of Babel that had wooed the workmen back into its bowels to feed and clothe them, and give them all the "good" things of life, but still, very much like a pagan sacrificial altar stained, he had learned, with at least seven workmens' lives, barren of any lasting contribution except to someone's ego—just there.

It was an instant revelation, this hopeless striving of man; and what he had just done was the only answer to their dilemma, their lostness. And yet, it wasn't him, really, but a power that had used him and had given him an almost overwhelming burden for them. And sitting there in his cab, his hands tightly gripping the wheel, he finally knew what he wanted to do with the rest of his life.

Gradually, his boldness grew and he ventured out at night to talk to street gangs or prostitutes. Often he would come in late, weary and discouraged, to find Amy eager to learn how it had gone and ready to encourage.

"You know, hon," she said one night, "I think what you're doing is great, but maybe it would be a lot easier if you weren't alone. Maybe if we joined a church and you had support...someone to go with you. Isn't

16

that what the body is all about?"

So they started attending a nearby Bible church. But though people smiled and shook hands, there were stares at Scott's shoulder length hair and Amy's long, hand sewn dresses. Scott repeatedly invited some of the younger men to go with him to the streets, but they always had excuses.

They visited other churches. Some offered great sermons that fed their intellects. Some, entertainment by "professional" Christian musicians hired with "love offerings." But the deep spiritual needs they both had were not met.

Consequently, one Sunday morning Scott decided they would have "church" at home. While the baby slept, he, Amy and little David gathered around the oak coffee table Scott had made, read the Bible, prayed and sang songs. Scott strummed his guitar with relish. Just as they were finishing, someone knocked at the door.

"Hello there, Scott." He recognized two ladies from the Bible church.

"Come in," he said, smiling.

Fern and Doris, both in their late forties, carried large Bibles. They looked around the flat, decorated with stacked orange crates for book shelves, at Amy's macramé and plants hanging everywhere amidst an incongruous antique collection. Scott decided not to offer them bean bags and brought two chairs from the kitchen.

"My, what an unusual candlestick," Fern said, walking to the silver rococo styled holder on the buffet.

"Yes, it's my favorite piece," Amy said.

The ladies sat down. "Well, Doris and I just thought we'd drop in for a moment after church and see how you two were doing. We haven't seen you for awhile,"

17

Fern said.

"Yeah, well, we thought we'd visit other churches," Scott answered. "But that hasn't worked out too well so we, just this morning, decided to have our own service,"

Doris and Fern looked at each other.

"That's fine," Doris said, "But the Bible does say we shouldn't forsake ourselves from joining one another..."

"And also," Fern straightened her skirt, "a home Bible study is fine, but only as a supplement to the church. A new Christian needs the fellowship of other Christians. He needs care and help over rough spots, just like a little baby."

Scott cleared his throat.

Amy said quickly, "We're not really new Christians."

"Of course," Fern added, "and now you need the meat of the word, not the milk, and the best place to find that is in church."

Scott began to fidget. "You know," he said, very deliberately, "sermons have never built my faith half as much as having to walk into a dark alley alone and see the Lord work mightily with a bunch of drunken bikers."

"Well," Fern continued, "I believe you're just asking for trouble when you go out alone. The Lord said to go out, two by two."

"I agree. And if no one wants to go?"

The women looked at each other again. Doris studied her watch. "My, we'll miss our ride," she said. "Promise you will come and visit us once in awhile."

"You never know," Scott answered, but he knew he wouldn't be back. He continued working the streets and bars, going back often to certain clubs for which he felt a particular burden. When the bartenders realized he wasn't pushy with patrons, they softened toward him and even bought him orange juice, "on the house." Often he ran into the petite blonde, Irene, who began to open up to him.

"Do you have a church?" she asked one day.

"No. We have church in our home, just my family."

"Sounds cool. Do you ever invite people to come?"

"I haven't thought about it. Why, would you like to?"

"When do you have it?"

"Sunday morning."

Irene's face fell. I'm a waitress, I have to work everyday but Monday."

All the next week, Scott thought about what she had said. Most of the people he was trying to reach in the neighborhood—show people, bartenders, waitresses never worked on Monday because it was a slow night for business. With Amy's approval, he went to a neighborhood printer and ordered five hundred calling cards. The copy read, "Got problems? Life going nowhere fast? Need a change? Meetings every Monday night, 7:00 p.m., 1632 N. Sedgwick."

He began passing out the cards wherever he went. For the first month no one showed, then Irene and a younger girl she worked with arrived one Monday night.

Delighted, Scott kept things loose, singing songs they would know like *Amazing Grace*. They talked about life and read the Bible some, and the women promised to return.

They did, and others came—mostly street people, young and searching. Some came out of a kind of hell where having experiences with demons while "tripping" happened often. Many were skeptical when they first received Scott's card, thinking he was pushing another cult like the Krishnas' or Moonies'. When they found Scott's Jesus loved them just the way they were, that in due time, *He* would deliver them from *all* enslaving habits, that they couldn't do it themselves by becoming "religious," that all they had to do was surrender, they responded. Like one beggar telling another beggar where to find bread, they spread the word that Jesus had come to town with a basket big enough for everybody. And Scott began to dream big.

His hardest job was getting them to open up to each other. Admittedly, the meetings sounded like Alcoholic Anonymous, at times, but at the end of three months, they packed Scott's two-room apartment, wall to wall. They called themselves "Maranatha" and some of the younger men even put on black robes and pounded staffs against the sidewalk in protest outside strip bars. There was no sacred ground. People coming out of sport arenas, shopping malls, even out of churches, were presented with the Gospel.

Local pastors, uncomfortable with their fanaticism, treated them as though they had the plague. Their answer? "Before you come down heavy on our unorthodox ways, at least be as sold out as we are." They pointed out that all the real "doers" in the history of Christianity were the fanatics of their day—St. Francis, Luther, Finney, and most of all, Jesus. That, in a fanatical society where people scream their lungs out at a ball game or beat each other up at a hockey game, it sometimes took a fanatic to get attention; and that, for far too long, Christians had fought a defensive war, using the name of Jesus apologetically.

"We are called to war," Scott would say, "to fight spiritual warfare. If we don't fight aggressively we will become a prisoner of war. If we're not in the army of God, we're in the jail house of the devil."

But the night Carmen showed up, Scott would long remember. Smart, always wisecracking, con man Carmen. Scott had met him at "His" place on Rush St. where he tended bar. Through their many late night talks, Scott learned that little mattered to the good-looking Italian except a foxy lady and his gun collection. Though he didn't have a permit, he always kept a loaded Colt .45 under the counter "just in case." A star quarterback at Lane Technical High School, he was offered scholarships, but lacked motivation. Now at 33, he was a drifter, living for little more than another sexual conquest.

During the meeting he sat near the window, looking out at the people below, as Scott tried to show how relevant the Gospel was to the problems of life.

"That sounds slick as snot," Carmen smirked suddenly. "But tell us about Swaggart and Jim Bakker. I read the other day that Barbie doll is divorcing Bakker for his best friend."

Everyone waited for Scott to respond, but he wasn't ready for the challenge. He had wondered, himself, how these men could destroy the confidence of millions of followers by giving in to temptations of the flesh. But he had already concluded earlier that it was wrong to judge them—his own life history forbade it.

He took a deep breath, searching hard for an answer that was honest without sounding trite. "One time they brought a woman to Jesus who got caught in adultery," he began. "They were going to stone her to death, the usual punishment. But Jesus knew half the guys there had probably slept with her, so, he reaches down, picks up a stone, and holding it out, says, 'who here is worthy to cast the first stone?"'

Carmen said nothing more the rest of the evening and started showing up regularly to the meetings. One night, six months later, he told everyone that he had decided to become a Christian. Scott didn't know what to think, but the changes in the man in the following months were undeniable. Except for his guns—he still kept a loaded .45 under the bar.

One Monday night Doris and Fern returned. The group sized them up, then ignored them. The two women sat in a corner, tight lipped and apprehensive. Scott watched their reaction to the vocal worship of the street people and relished in their bewilderment, proud of what his little home church had become. He hoped they got the point.

It was when Amy's big silver goblet filled with wine was being passed for the Lord's supper that he first received the thought. He tried to reject it, but then it came again, along with a certain memory. It was six months earlier and he was sitting in Fern and Doris's Church, feeling alone and out of place.

While everyone was still worshipping, he went to the kitchen and filled a pan with lukewarm water. Finding a clean wash cloth and towel, he went back into the living room and knelt before Doris. It was a warm night, and both ladies were wearing sandals. He unfastened the straps and gently washed their feet.

THREE

Lieutenant John Ramsey eased his six-foot, four-inch frame onto his favorite stool at the end of Gino's counter. "Big John," as he was known by the men under him, poured cream into his coffee and checked the race results in the morning edition one more time.

He had done a stupid thing yesterday. He had bet five hundred on a horse his sergeant said belonged to a rich relative who was holding the horse back to make a killing in yesterday's race. The horse finished fifth.

He lit a cigarette. Maybe the wife was right. He had to have been sick to have taken all their vacation money and just thrown it away like that. He stirred the coffee slowly, thinking about it. Still, no one's perfect, he told himself. Sometimes it paid in life to take a chance. At eight to one, "Blue Lady" would have returned him a tidy twenty thousand, just enough for a small resort he hoped to have when he retired.

Yeah, but this time he was in deep. Lee had called a lawyer the last time she caught him and had promised, complete with waving bread knife, that there would be no "next time." So why had he done it? Was she right that he had a disease as surely as those men with a dope habit his men busted daily? No, he couldn't buy that. What then? Deep down, he knew it wasn't the money. Perhaps he relished a little spice in a bored life of endless riding in squads or shuffling tons of paper work. But he didn't play around. He didn't drink to excess. As a young daredevil cop, he had a reputation for being fearless. But that was a long time back. Now, he was three years away from retirement, wore both upper and lower dental plates, and as of yesterday's loss, was almost flat broke.

He was putting down the second cup when his driver came hurrying in.

"Lieutenant, headquarters is trying to reach you— some nut's hanging on a cross in front of the Picasso."

"What? For cryin' out loud. What next?" Throwing some change on the counter, the lieutenant grabbed his hat and paper and headed for the squad.

They sped the six blocks to the Civic Center, not using siren or lights because of the light traffic. They screeched to a halt on the Dearborn Street side of the plaza. A group of six or seven people stood around a man wearing a burlap bag for a shirt and faded Levi's, hung up on an eight-foot cross that appeared to have been cut from a large tree limb. The lieutenant grabbed his night stick and hat and hoisted his large frame out of the black and white compact Ford.

His trained eyes quickly scanned Scott's thin frame, long hair, and the hardened steel chains with heavy locks around his wrists and ankles. Scott wasn't hanging from the chains, a small platform supported most of his weight. Now he stared down at the officer, his lips tightly pressed together.

"May I ask..." the lieutenant began.

"Officer, we have a permit," said Carmen, stepping forward and waving a slip of paper.

Big John read the permit issued by the Civic Center management office. It gave permission for a religious service to be held on the plaza from Friday through Easter Sunday by the group called "Maranatha." It was signed by the plaza manager. He handed it back to Carmen, and at the same time, looked him over—from the bare feet in sandals, to the faded Levi's, to the tee shirt with "Jesus is Lord" across the chest, to the dark wavy hair and manicured mustache.

"What are you guys, some kinda cult?"

"No sir," Carmen answered quickly. "Not a cult. We just love Jesus."

"Is this your idea of a religious service?"

"Well, yes."

"What do you hope to accomplish?"

Carmen began to explain about the true meaning of Easter. Though the lieutenant appeared to be listening, he was thinking about what the captain's reaction would be. When Carmen finished, he said, "You got fifteen minutes to get him down, and if you don't take him down, we will." He turned and walked briskly back to his car. "Get Quincy," he told the driver.

"Quincy's checked out," the female dispatcher reported back over the radio.

"Get him at home and patch me into him," the lieutenant barked to the driver. As he waited for the connection, Lieutenant Ramsey fumed. Quincy was supposed to pass the plaza every thirty minutes. The plaza was the pride of the city, a showplace for out-of-towners visiting on vacation, to gawk at the Picasso sculpture or the six story Christmas tree and ice sculptures during winter. It needed to be watched constantly for unauthorized demonstrators and vandals. If he found out Quincy had been shacking up with that Spanish broad again, he'd suspend him for thirty days, and without pay.

"Lieutenant, Quincy's on the line," purred the female voice. "Go ahead, Lieutenant."

"Quincy?"

"Yes, Lieutenant."

"There's a guy down here at the Civic Center hanging on a cross. How did this loony get by you?"

"Well, they got a permit, I looked it over..."

"For a religious service, not a damn exhibition," the lieutenant barked quickly.

"I know but...something else."

"Yeah, what?"

"When I tried to move 'em out, the kid with the permit claimed he called all the TV stations and newspapers and that they were going to show up this morning. He started tellin' me that he was going to fill their ears with police harassment and I didn't think I should push it till I checked with you. It's in my report."

Lieutenant Ramsey sat holding the mike to his lips, his mouth formed to speak. The driver sat staring straight ahead, his hands gripping the wheel, the soft whir of the motor idling, the only sound in the car.

The lieutenant vividly recalled the clamor made by various minority groups over the past three months, claiming police brutality and harassment when they had demonstrated at the plaza. Some ambitious rookies had made it rough for the department by busting several without even determining if they had permits. He had been ordered to the Mayor's office to give an explanation. He didn't need to go through that again.

At last, he pressed the mike button. "Okay, Quincy, you got a point." He handed the mike to the driver. "Headquarters," he barked, and the driver pulled out into traffic. "The kid can have his day till I hear from higher up."

Carmen watched the squad pull away, then turned to Scott. "What should we do?"

"Nothing. We're staying. What time is it?"

"Almost seven. Many people get Good Friday off, but there'll be some action anyway, I bet."

By nine, the Plaza was a hub of activity, mostly office workers, young secretaries dressed in latest fashion, young executives in Brooks Brothers suits, with fancy leather brief cases, all hurrying in different directions, intent, focused, and refusing to look at Scott. A few more members of Maranatha arrived, and now they all began to sing—the songs of their fellowship, Israeli fight songs, songs from the Psalms. A few curious street people stopped, but mostly Scott's group was ignored by the throngs bustling by.

When the singers stopped, Carmen looked up at Scott.

"Would you believe it? We're not making a dent."

"Preach," Scott said. "The cross convicts them; that's why they won't look at us."

"What do I say? I've never done it before."

"Just start, the words will come. Better yet, read II Chronicles 7:14."

Carmen opened his Bible. "This is the word of the God of Abraham, Isaac, and Jacob..."

"Louder," Scott interrupted.

"If my people who are called by my name will humble themselves, pray, seek my face, and turn from their wicked ways, then will I hear from Heaven, forgive their sin, and heal their land." Carmen paused.

"Again." Scott said.

So Carmen read it again, and at Scott's urging, kept reading it repeatedly. Each time his voice grew stronger until it echoed across the plaza. The Maranatha people had spread out and were distributing large numbers of the tract Scott had written, "The Real Meaning of Easter."

Nobody from the press approached them as they continued to sing and pass out literature throughout the morning. By noon, Scott's lower back, shoulders, and arms were killing him. And he thought of the verse, "I will not offer to the Lord that which cost me nothing."

At 1:30, a squad car pulled up opposite them. Sergeant Quincy got out of the car, put on his black and white checkered hat and walked briskly to the cross. Quincy was short and round with a red complexion and wore a very crisp uniform.

"Well hello again," Carmen smiled.

Quincy wasn't smiling. "You fellows will have to give it up. I just got a call from the lieutenant."

"But you saw our permit."

"It's been revoked. Mayor Daley wants you gone. You got twenty minutes. I'm going for coffee across the street. You better not be here when I get back."

"And if we are?" Carmen was not smiling now.

"I call a swat team who will bring a torch. After they cut you down, we take you in and book you."

"On what charge?" Carmen demanded.

"Vagrancy and refusing to obey a police officer for starters," Quincy said over his shoulder.

When he was gone, Carmen raised his voice in derision. "Can you beat that? Offer him a C-note and we'd be here to Christmas." As he started to pace restlessly, the Maranatha people gathered around, concern showing in their faces. Someone suggested a prayer. As they prayed, Scott's thoughts began to crystallize. He had planned this event for six months, this had been no last minute whim. His society had turned Easter into a pagan holiday, an excuse to spend on stuffed bunnies and fancy threads. He was well aware that the early church never celebrated Christ's resurrection, that the Roman church had turned a pagan worship of Estre, the goddess of spring, into a Christian event. But his society didn't know that. So he had decided to use it as one more way to prick its conscience.

He had watched them hurrying by all morning, so intent, so anxious to worship the great whore of commerce, to receive from her shiny new playthings in exchange for their souls.

When some did look up at him, they would look away quickly; some even reacted as though they had been struck. Scott knew his presence on the Plaza had made a difference. His being on the cross not fifty feet from the large Picasso sculpture was so out of context, so bizarre, its shock value had to be enormous.

But he had not yet accomplished his goal—to stay on the cross for three days, and each day until dark, and he wasn't about to give up so soon. The praying had ended. They were all looking up at him, waiting his direction.

"You guys take off. You, too, Carmen. I'm staying," he told them.

Some objected, but he was adamant, and one by one they left—only Carmen remained.

"There's no reason you need to get busted, too. They sound serious now. You better go," Scott told him.

"Is that right?" Carmen snapped. "You know, since I've known you, you've had an attitude."

"What?"

"You heard me. You're a loner. You never let anyone get close to you, to give you a hand."

"So, what's the point?"

"The point is, I'm in this thing, too. You helped me big time, I ain't about to walk out on you now, so don't pull that stuff about obeying an elder, either."

Scott studied the face of his friend. Most of the time Carmen controlled his emotions, but when he was really steamed, his eyes betrayed him. They were glaring coals now.

"O.K. You got a record?"

"Funny you should ask."

"What did you do?"

"It was stupid. I took a couple of joints to school when I was a kid. The teacher turned me in. I did 90 days in a work camp."

"I don't think it will matter much one way or the other. Just watch what you say. You don't have to make it any harder on us by an attitude. We go peaceable, right?"

"Gotcha."

True to his word, Quincy was back in twenty minutes. He sat in his car talking on his radio. After awhile, a blue windowless van drove up. Dressed in black, wearing bulletproof vests and riot helmets, six swat team members poured out of the van as if ready to do battle with terrorists.

"I don't believe it," Carmen laughed.

"Cool it."

One of them had a portable acetylene outfit. Another carried a ladder. Led by Quincy, they approached the two.

"Well, what's it gonna' be? You comin' down?" Quincy asked.

Scott shook his head. The swat team went right to work. Setting the ladder in place, one climbed it, put on dark goggles, and began to cut the chain from Scott's left wrist. He worked on the back side of the wood so as not to burn Scott.

Now the crowd they had longed for began to gather, and soon, a hundred or so surrounded them. A wino, stretched out on a nearby concrete bench awoke, raised up on an elbow and yelled, "Leave 'em be, why don't ya. You're a bunch of goons, you got no Easter spirit." And he lay down again.

In no time at all, the team had Scott down and were putting the cuffs on both of them.

They were booked in at 11th and State headquarters, but due to crowded conditions, were taken with four black gang members in a van to Cook County jail at 26th and California.

FOUR

Lenny Blackman, Scott's roommate in cell block C-4, paused to light a cigarette. "So I watched the car pull away and I saw her looking back through the rear window as long as she could and I wondered if she was crying, too. You guys can't, in your wildest dreams, know the pain I felt. But there was nothing I could do, the man had a warrant. He said she was a truant from school, a drug user and a runaway. It happened just before Thanksgiving. She had just turned fourteen.

"Me, and the wife and kids tried to have fun that Thanksgiving, but we quit pretending. Now that I think about it, I should have given the kids more individual attention when they were younger. I saw a Girl Scout poster one time that read, 'the time to worry about an eighteen-year old is when she's eight.' How true that is."

It was the third day after their appearance in court, in which Scott and Carmen received 15-day sentences for resisting a police officer. Amy had come to court somewhat anxious; but when they said good-bye, she smiled encouragement and he knew she'd be okay. Now, Scott, Carmen and Lenny were sitting at a table in one corner of the day room as the men around them, mostly young blacks, played cards or watched TV.

Lenny Blackman was in his mid-forties and was a long haul truck driver. He was a big man with a bushy black beard and huge tattooed forearms. Everyone in the block gave him plenty of space, but he was not an intimidator. Scott found him to be sensitive and well read, especially about politics. He read the Bible often and referred to himself as a "constitutionalist." Scott knew the type from listening to short-wave, extremely patriotic, insisting Congress abide by the Constitution. Lenny had been arrested for "kidnapping" his own daughter.

"I don't get it," Scott said. "How could the government just take her out of your home?"

"You would be amazed at the stuff I've learned since this thing with Jennifer started. You better not lay a hand on your kid today...don't get me wrong, I seldom did. But if your kid or your neighbor calls that family welfare service with a complaint, you can easily end up in the slammer for child abuse."

"You went to court, right?"

"Yeah. We got a five minute hearing in the judge's chambers. That's another thing, these kind of cases never get heard in public. Jennifer sat in a chair beside the judge, wearing patched jeans, truckin' boots, and her brother's blue work shirt. She kept looking down, her face hidden by her long brown hair. The assistant D.A. was doing all the talking. First, he asks her if she feels the rules at home are too strict. 'Yes', she mumbles so low you could hardly hear her. Then he asks her if she would run again if she were put back into our home.

"'Yes,' she answers again. The judge ruled she was a neglected minor whose behavior was injurious to her welfare, and puts her in a foster home."

"What was her beef?" Carmen wanted to know.

"The wife blamed me. I admit I was tough on my kids. When I told them to move, they moved. That's the way my Pa raised me, so I figured that's how I should raise mine. She was the second youngest of five closely spaced kids and got lost in the crowd. She's headstrong, just like her old man. And she probably had more needs than the others but I didn't pick up on it, I was gone so much. I wish now I'd seen it. Her street friends saw it and took advantage.

"I did wake up eventually. I saw something one day driving my truck through a suburb of Chicago. Jennifer had run away from that foster home the judge put her in, and the wife and I were going nuts with worry. You never knew if you might get a call late some night that she had overdosed, or got done in by some creep she had hitched a ride from. She used to hitchhike a lot."

"So she runs again," Carmen interjected, "even after she got her wish and got out from under you. So obviously, there had to be more going on, right?"

"Well, that's what my wife and I thought. If she had been allowed to come home, we could have worked out our differences somehow, which we eventually did. But Big Brother wouldn't hear. Big Brother had psychologists and other experts who know all about family relationships, except they don't have a very good track record in patching up families.

"You know, for the longest time I just didn't see it. I was a good provider, I treated all the kids fairly and I thought I loved them, but then this thing happened in Elmhurst. I was sitting in my rig at this stoplight, cussing my heater because I was slowly turning into an icicle, when I noticed that the kids were getting out of school across the street. A white-haired guard, wearing an old army coat and an American Legion cap, was taking those kids across the street in a long line when he stops and buttons the coat of a little blond tyke about eight years old. He was talking at the little thing who could steal you heart with one look, and you know he was giving it to her for running out of school all unwrapped.

"The guy behind me is laying on his horn but there's nothing I could do, so I leaned out the door and politely told him so. Then I get the smarts—the old duffer had control of the lights. Traffic is starting to back up both ways and the horns are blaring, but I wasn't going to bust no light—not in that town.

"Well, the old maestro takes the white fur cap the little tyke is carrying and puts it on her head. But first, he has to get all those strands of corn silk tucked underneath, and in order to do that, he has to take off a glove and put it in his pocket. The horns are making enough racket to rupture the old guy's hearing aid, but he doesn't know a thing.

"Finally, he's finished. But, get this, before he can straighten up, this little kid throws her arms around his neck and gives him a big smack.

"After he pushed the button and we were on our way, I watched in my side mirror as long as I could. Every one of those kids had a wave or smile for the old man as they passed.

"All the rest of that day I'm bugged, and I can't figure out why. I mean, that old dude could have hurried her and the others along so he could get home to his hot bowl of soup and maybe a TV soap opera. But he took time to help her so she wouldn't catch cold. He could care less about the rat race everybody's running today. When that little thing threw her arms around his neck, something hit me right here. It had been a long

35

time since my kids kissed me like that old boy got kissed." Lenny paused, obviously fighting back emotion. He lit another cigarette.

"So, that week I quit my job and started looking for local hauling. I started getting home at supper and quit going to the local bar. And I saw a change in the kids from the git-go."

"What about Jennifer?" Carmen asked.

"Well, Christmas was coming on and we were all hoping we'd hear something from her. For all we knew, she could be in Canada, or Mexico, or at a friend's, three blocks away. So we just made our plans and went back to pretending, but we knew there's no way it would be the same.

"I remembered all the Christmas mornings when Jennifer and her sisters would come tripping into the front room in their too large sleeper pajamas, gibbering excitedly over all the gifts.

"Well, that night, after everyone had gone to bed, the wife and I sat up awhile sipping some wine in front of the fire and thinking about Jennifer, if she was okay, and all. Then the wife turned in and I sat alone, just thinking.

"Sometime after midnight there was soft knocking at the front door. I went to it and there I see the sorriest looking kid in the world—blue jeans dragged in mud, her face haggard. Snow was falling, the big fluffy kind, and her hair was covered with it. She looked older.

"'I came home for Christmas,' she says. 'I can leave if you want, I got a place.'

"I give her a big hug and take her over to the fire. She's shivering and she's soaked. She sits down and tries to untie her truckin' boots, but she couldn't do it. She was too beat. She must have walked a long way, too proud to call us to come get her. I got the boots off and her wet woolen socks, lay them by the fire, and headed upstairs to get the wife.

"'Wait a minute, huh?' she says.

"'Okay,'" I says. 'How 'bout I make some Ovaltine?' She loved Ovaltine, especially with marshmallows. I made some and we sat there awhile and I didn't know what to say. After some time the sniffling began. As always, you couldn't see her face behind her hair.

"'I quit smoking,' she says real proud like.

"'That's good,' I say, and I start to ask her about dope, but catch myself. She tells me she's got lots of things inside her head that she's got to get out. She's sick of the hassles between us and thinks that I think she is totally immature and out to impress, or just rebel by finding a freak with dope. I just let her ramble because I don't know what to say, anyway.

"She says she doesn't want to go back to the state home which is where she's headed, but I haven't got the nerve to say it. She's looking up at me, tears washing mascara down her cheek. She tells me she dreamed one night I was shouting at her, calling her a slut. She admitted her values were distorted with drugs and sex, that, at one time, she thought friends could be the same as family. But now she's not so sure. Something happened that changed her mind.

"When she didn't go on for some time I figured I better say it. I mean, her eyes dug into me for just a shred of evidence she wouldn't be hurt again. I said to her, 'Jennifer, would you forgive me for not being the dad I should have been to you, for not being around when you needed me, for being too busy with my job, and a thousand other things?'

"She wouldn't look at me, wouldn't answer. I had to get her to see it would be different, that I had changed, that I knew she was older and wiser than her years and would try to treat her differently. I told her that I loved her just the way she was and never again would I try to change her. I wanted to say much more but I couldn't. I broke down. I don't think she ever saw her old man bawl before.

"Well, she comes over to me and sits down very close on the sofa and lays her head on my chest and her tears and mascara are messing up my new Christmas shirt, but it didn't matter. We sat there awhile watching the fire and then I asked her what was it that happened that changed her mind.

"She tells me she had been riding around with a bunch of kids she was staying with in a town in Wisconsin. It was late at night and they were partying at a park and were watching this old drunk sitting under a street light. She said he looked very loncly, he just sat there staring at the ground. He had long hair and a white beard, his clothes looked worked over—his pants were covered with patches. Her friends laughed at him, making jokes about the wine bottle in his hand.

"She says they were on their third case of beer, had smoked a lot of pot earlier, rock was blasting from the radio.

"Then she said she noticed her friend, sitting next to her in the back seat, wasn't laughing. He says to her, 'I better go get my old man' and he stumbles out of the car and over to the man. He tries to pick him up, but the two are too drunk to get anything accomplished. Nobody in the car is laughing now, they're surprised by their friend's actions.

"She said she got out of the car and helped her friend pick the old man up. When the two were on their way, she gets back in, and they all watched the two stagger down the street, arm in arm.

"'It's his pa,' she told them, but she says they just turned up the music and peeled off—drunk and laughing—to get some more beer. And, for whatever reason, that was the turning point for her.

"Well, for a couple days it was great her being home, but I knew it was just a matter of time before the state got wind she was back and would come and get her. We had a family pow-wow and it seemed best if her and I took a little vacation. I had an old drinking buddy who had gone to Arkansas and built a cabin in the woods to get away from it all, so we headed down there.

"On the way down, I'm toolin' down the interstate in Missouri and a trooper pulls me over for a burned out tail light. He runs a check and finds a warrant has been put out on Jennifer."

"Talk about rotten luck," Scott sympathized.

"Tell me about it. Jennifer was really bummed out. I'm sure they got her locked up good and tight now."

"That poor kid."

For awhile the three sat watching the TV, each lost in his own thoughts.

"So they got you on kidnapping your own kid," Carmen said, finally.

"That's it," Lenny agreed. "Crossing the state line is what did it."

"How much time you facing?"

"From what I hear it's all up to the judge. If I can convince him I was acting in the best interest of the kid, I might get a wrist slap or I might get five years. But you better believe I'd do it again."

That night Scott lay in his bunk thinking of Lenny's story which hadn't startled him. From his short-wave listening he had heard many testimonies about out of control government agencies. He called short-wave the country's underground communication system, where call-in talk shows were uncensored, where victims of the IRS, BATF and other agencies had a chance to air their side of the story, the kind of stuff you never heard from T.V.'s Ted Koppel.

Lenny's claim that government agencies were victimizing innocent people was not news to him. One investigator had reported at least a million families had experienced unnecessary hurt at the government's hands. Families had been split up, children drugged and interned, or put into foster homes where, quite often, real child abuse occurred. Parents were often jailed—all because someone made a complaint which, too frequently, was unsubstantiated.

He wondered, too, why the media seldom reported agency abuses. But let some poor slob get caught evading taxes and he got all kinds of coverage, especially at tax time. Apparently, the media was being controlled, but by what, or whom, he wondered?

In the past three years he had watched America change. The moral decay that seemed to be spreading, like a raging fire out of control, was apparent everywhere, especially in government. There was a definite trend toward socialism, where government interfered in private life and seemed to have an agenda to wipe out small businesses through over regulation and tax burdens.

Some said the President was to blame. Some blamed the Congress; everyone had someone else to fault except himself. No one seemed to understand that government was a reflection of society. He remembered the bumper sticker that read, "We've got the best government money can buy," and it occurred to him that corruption just didn't spring up in one day. It grew slowly and gradually from the first time a campaign contribution was accepted, or a lobbyist greased a palm under the table, and John Q. could care less because he had his own hand out.

Now he wondered about the future. Many were predicting a market crash. Some of the callers to the short-wave talk shows spoke of a global conspiracy by international bankers to reduce the wealth of the country, so desperate Americans would give up freedoms and willingly accept a one world government, where nations merged together "for economic security."

One of his favorite subjects in school had been history. He could remember being excited reading how just a handful of patriots endured great dangers to finally overpower the stronger British forces because they were willing to risk everything, rather than become slaves.

While the vast majority pretended that the cares of daily living were more than enough to fret about, it was the few, he reflected, who changed the course of history—dedicated, tough, willing to fight to the death for a cause they believed in.

And sometimes, the few became only one. One, with a vision of the future, a seer with guts, a nonconformist who cared little for social acceptance, but couldn't rest because he saw his society plunging headlong into disaster, being wooed by the piper to a wrong gospel, or wrong "ism," because it was too lazy, or uncaring, or desensitized by liberal education or TV propaganda.

Many Christians in the country were saying that all the prophecies of Christ's second coming had been fulfilled, that He could come at any time. He wasn't sure of that, but he was feeling an increased sense of urgency, and that night he slept very little.

"Lenny, let me ask you a question," he addressed

the big man at breakfast. "Do you believe America's under judgment?"

"I know it is," Lenny said emphatically.

"You think AIDS is part of it?"

"It fits Matthew 24, doesn't it, where it talks about pestilence? The Master said that wars, famines, earthquakes and pestilences would all increase just before He comes back, remember?"

"I know that, but you don't think he would lay AIDS on the people, do you?"

"I don't know, He might," Lenny said.

"I don't think He would," Scott said. "The way I like to think of it is that we are sheep. If we stray out of God's corral, out from under His protection, we can be picked off by wolves. AIDS is basically spread by homosexuals and dope users and both life styles oppose God's law, the way I read my Bible."

"And what about innocent victims who get it?" That was one of the characteristics in Lenny that Scott found annoying. He liked to play the devil's advocate.

"Well, for that matter, why do innocents suffer at all?" Scott answered. "I fought with that one for a long time and then I gave it up because it was beyond me. All I could ever come up with was that He gave society rules to live by, rules for our own protection. When we violate these rules by starting wars, coveting our neighbor's wife, or whatever, we suffer the consequences, and our children suffer right along with us."

"I can't argue that. But I'll tell you one thing, there's a lot more to this pestilence business than anybody realizes."

"How so?"

"From what I understand, there's a whole new generation of viruses killing a lot of folks all over the world. Stuff like Ebola Zaire, Hanta Virus and new strains of tuberculosis that's driving the doctors crazy. I mean, we're not talking a few hundred a month, but thousands per day! Ever hear of the Desert Storm Syndrome?"

"No."

"Well, hold on to your seat. Vets who were in Desert Storm started getting sick when they got back—not only them, but their families, too. Seven thousand have died so far and thousands more are real sick."

"What do they have?"

"Weird stuff like flu symptoms that get gradually worse, even strange types of cancer, but they don't know whether its a virus, bacteria or radiation poison causing it. One doctor who has treated a lot of these guys believes millions of Americans have already been infected because it's so contagious."

"So how come the government hasn't said anything?"

"No one knows. The Department of Defense is playing deaf and dumb, telling the vets it's in their heads. But there's a lot of hard evidence that the vets were exposed to experimental inoculation by our government and to germ warfare in Desert Storm. Guess who sold Iraq germ warfare weapons just before that war started? Our government."

"It's pretty hard for me to swallow our government would do that."

"I understand. Just don't forget, twenty years ago they lied about spraying our guys with Agent Orange in Nam, or that they experimented with LSD on young privates. And before that, that they injected pregnant women and babies with plutonium. Heck, you can read about the Gulf War stuff in a report put out by the Senate Veterans' Affairs Committee. It's called, 'Is Military Research Hazardous to Veterans' Health?'

Even that report claims the Department of Defense used the vets as guinea pigs for experimental drugs and vaccines."

"Incredible, Lenny, just incredible. How could they do it—these are their own people?"

"Tell me about it. The only thing I can come up with is that those creeps pushing the New World Order are behind it, somehow. They've said publicly, many times, that a drastic population reduction is a key element in their plan for an eventual world government."

"You know, Lenny, regardless of who's pulling the strings, Christ's warnings about pestilence is unfolding right before our eyes."

"Right on. And you better know He's got the answer for us to get through all this. But each of us better be listening real hard. He's been trying to get our attention for a long time. He may only speak once.

FIVE

In the remaining days of their sentence, Scott and Carmen talked a lot to Lenny, continually amazed at the extent of his knowledge of critical world issues. Like Scott, Lenny also owned a short-wave receiver and had been an avid listener for years. He had memorized the Constitution and once stood up in a town meeting and asked the two senators on stage if either one could recite at least six of the ten Bill of Rights. Neither could. Lenny's family had been stockpiling food, gasoline, all the essentials, for the last couple of years, convinced the country was headed toward chaos.

"You know," Carmen said, "before Clinton, I would have thought you were nuts. But when he got in, something happened to the morale of the country—people have no trust in government at all these days. All my gun buddies are boiling mad about the Brady Bill and the Crime Bill getting ramrodded through congress."

"You don't know the half of it," Lenny said. "People in the know say very few congressmen even read the Crime Bill, that it wasn't available in a complete form when they voted. It contains all sort of government liberties—house to house searches without a warrant, seizure of private property if drug involvement is even suspected.

"They're playing right into the hands of the global-ists, knowingly or not. They're probably so blinded by their self-serving lusts, they don't see they're selling America down the river, demoralizing the people, throwing sand into the gears of our economy..."

"And they're coming after our guns," Carmen inter-jected.

"Of course. In the New World Order, each country signs away its sovereignty, each citizen of that country loses individual freedoms, like owning a gun. You know, you can't enslave an armed man. Hitler and Sta-lin knew that. That's why the very first thing they did when they came into power was to disarm the people."

"They ain't going to get mine," Carmen said de-fiantly.

"What will you do?" Scott quietly asked. "Kill the officer who comes through your door looking for your guns? Jesus said if you live by the sword, you die by the sword."

"Then, I guess I die by the sword," Carmen said. "What's right is right."

"There are a lot of people in the country who agree with him," Lenny said to Scott. "A lot of people were sitting on the fence until the Randy Weaver thing happened..."

"You mean the guy in Idaho who got set up by the government? What really happened there?" Scott asked.

"Make you sick," Lenny said. "400 troops, millions spent, the guy loses his son and pregnant wife—all over a shotgun barrel an informant convinces him to shorten. Here's a guy who didn't bother anyone. Nice, wholesome family that separated themselves from a world system that has abandoned true Christian values. They lived in the mountains, grew their own food, home schooled their children, had many friends in the area.

"As the story goes, the Feds approached Weaver to help them find certain so called, 'extremist' families who owned guns. Weaver felt it was dishonorable to spy on fellow citizens for the government and told them so. They told him that if he didn't cooperate they would set him up, put him in jail and he would lose his home.

"Over a year later the family is still on their place, afraid to go out, any food or stuff they needed, not supplied by their garden, friends brought. Then in August of '92, eight U.S. Marshals converge on the place. The dog smells them and gives out a yelp and they shoot it.

Weaver, his friend, and his 14 year-old son grab rifles when they hear the shot and head out. The son is shot four times, Weaver's friend gets off a shot, but Weaver claims he never fired at them. A Marshall is killed by a single armor-piercing bullet through his bulletproof vest, but many people believe he was hit by his own team.

"So now we have a stand off. Martial Law is declared in two counties. Over 400 Feds are sent to the mountain, plus over 100 State Police. They bring in tanks, choppers, armored personnel carriers.

"A day or so later, Weaver, his friend and his 16 year-old daughter go to an outbuilding where Weaver's dead son is. They are unarmed but Weaver is shot in the back. His wife holds the door open for them and an FBI sniper, Lon Horiuchi, shoots her in the head. The 10-month old baby she's holding is miraculously not hurt, but fragments from the bullet and her skull hit

Weaver's friend in the chest, puncturing his lung and breaking a rib. Weaver slams the door and refuses to open it again.

"Meantime, the FBI clears out all the families living anywhere close. They set up a barricade at a bridge and people start coming in from all over the country. Over 250 men, women, and kids are camped at this bridge at Ruby Creek, as a vigil for justice. Ministers and friends of the Weavers plead with the FBI to let them go up and talk to Weaver, but they flat out refuse.

"The FBI places explosives around the house and a chopper loaded with diesel fuel is spotted headed toward the house, apparently to drop the stuff on the roof for a fire. A camera man from a local newspaper jumps out from under cover and waves his camera in the air until the pilot spots him and immediately flies away from the house. They arrest the cameraman for obstructing police work.

"Bo Gritz shows up, he was the most decorated guy in Nam. And guess what, he delivers a citizen's arrest warrant to the FBI, the Governor of Idaho, and the U.S. Marshal chief.

"Evidently it did some good because that day he was allowed up the mountain to talk to Weaver. When he came down that night, he told the crowd about Vicki's death and they about went into shock. They joined hands..." Lenny paused and took a deep breath and then said quietly, "they joined hands in a big circle in front of the barricade and prayed. People who were there say they will never forget it. People were sobbing and crying out to God, and then someone began to yell 'we're going to war.' Little did those goons watching from the other side have any notion what a dumb stunt they had pulled off.

"Well, after a few days, Bo got Weaver to give up and take his battle into the courts."

"What would have happened if he hadn't come down?" Carmen asked.

"Make no mistake. They would have fired the place."

"Like Waco?"

"Exactly. Get rid of the evidence, avoid anything that might prove embarrassing. After the siege, those goons cut off the wife's hands for finger prints and burned her remains. As far as I'm concerned, she did not die in defeat; she died in victory, standing for what she believed in.

"What happened at the trial?" Scott asked.

"In spite of all the lies put out by the government, Weaver was acquitted of all except two minor charges. The government was forced to pay $3.1 million for the wrongful deaths of two family members."

No one said anything for a long time. They sat, lost in thought, smoking their cigarettes, looking at the TV, oblivious of its message or the others around them.

"The way I see it," Lenny resumed after some time, "Christians are facing the greatest struggle they have ever had to face. We are up against the largest war machines, the worst bureaucracies, the most confusion, the most apathy, the most diabolical conspiracies possible. We are not going to pray these problems away, or be spared any of them.

"In my mind, God put us here at this time in history to face these problems with boldness and courage and to stand up against tyranny.

"What makes me sick to my stomach is the way the Christian big shots in this country reacted to the Weaver and Waco tragedies. So I didn't like the

Branch Davidians' theology, either, but by God, they had a right, under the Constitution, to preach it, and when they got hit like that, the churches and televangelists should have put up such a stink the government wouldn't have dared try it again. But who's making the stink these days—the patriots!

"There's always going to be guys like that around. Years ago it was the Birchers' or Goldwater's crowd, common people who just wanted the government to abide by the Constitution, but it took the Weaver and Waco massacres to wake up the country.

"Thank God for people like Linda Thompson, that lawyer from Indiana, and others who circulated VCR tapes of what really happened at Waco. They woke up a lot of folks. They show the government lied about child abuse, tons of munitions supposedly stored there, that the Branch Davidians all committed suicide by starting the blaze. The gas they pumped into that building for hours was inflammable and probably blinded everyone in there very quickly. They couldn't have found their way out, anyway. The FBI knew that. They knew the gas masks wouldn't fit the kids either."

"So, using child abuse as a reason to storm the place, Reno murders 17 little kids," Carmen sneered. "Now that's child abuse."

"Yes, my friend," Lenny said, sadly. "The consensus is, that certain government people used Waco as a test case to see how Americans would react."

"And they swallowed it whole," Carmen said.

"Right. But you have to understand, most people haven't the slightest notion how far the government will go. The first thing the FBI did was get the press two and a half miles back from the Waco site to conceal their actions. Then they fed the press all that B.S. and it got passed on to the people, word for word.

"The judge was totally prejudiced at the trial of the surviving Branch Davidians. Get this. He took it upon himself to pre-qualify the jury by mail. He asked them questions like, did they own guns, go to gun shows, what religion they were, whether they were Christians, so that he could sift out anyone who might not be sympathetic to the government's cause. This act was illegal—a gross violation of judicial practice, jurors don't have to answer these types of questions.

"In spite of all this rigging, and all the government lies at the trial, all the defendants were found innocent of conspiracy, or murder. By law, the jury had to find them guilty of possessing guns while a felony was being committed; but the jury wasn't concerned, thinking the sentence would be a slap on the wrist. So what does the judge rule? He sentences four of them a total of 240 years."

"Unbelievable," Carmen, exclaimed, slapping the table hard.

"Tell me about it. It's this kind of injustice that has so many people in this country ticked off. After Waco, people began forming militias in every state. And they're not supremist "skin heads" like the media wants us to believe—many are women, even grandmas who just want congress to obey the Constitution.

"Supposedly, the one-worlders were willing to wait for one more generation of kids indoctrinated with liberal, globalist brain-washing before they made their big move. But with the militia getting big so quickly, their agenda has been accelerated.

Scott shook his head, unbelieving. "What chance would the militia possibly have against tanks?"

"What chance did the Cong have against mighty America in Nam? What chance did the Afghanistans have against Russia? It's been proven many times throughout history that the side with heart has the advantage."

Scott was reminded immediately of the American Revolutionary War. But it had to be obvious that rifles alone, were hardly a match for government hi-tech ordnance in the hands of large numbers of well-trained troops.

"Do you really think," Scott asked, rubbing the five day stubble on his chin, "that American soldiers will be willing to fire on their own people?"

"They did at Kent College, remember? I understand U.S. Marines at the Twenty-nine Palms, California, Air-Ground Combat Center, were surveyed recently on whether they would be willing to kill American civilians who resisted giving up their guns. Sadly, a large percentage said they would. The Navy Seals were asked the same question."

"The way I see it, they're not going to gamble on whether some National Guard kid will fire on his own townspeople. The kid will be shipped overseas to be a policeman there, while we'll have Russians, Brazilians, or whatever, over here."

"You got any proof on that?" Scott asked.

"Hey, I seen the map put out by the Parliament for World Government. It shows the good Ol' U.S. being policed by Belgian, Russian, Columbian and Venezuelan troops. It shows our boys spread out all over the world, but none in this country.

"Right now they've got the states split up into ten regions. I remember region five is Minnesota, Wisconsin, Illinois, Ohio and two other states. Nixon established a Federal Regional Council for each region and put a chairman in each region who answers only to the President. Now get this...30 out of the 50 states have taken their boundaries out of their constitutions, which wipes out their sovereignty, when you think about it. And that's right in line with the agenda of the New World Order crowd."

"What the heck is this New World Order you're always talking about, anyway?" Carmen wanted to know.

"It's a buzz phrase for a scheme to enslave most of the world by the year 2000. The hype is that a global community, allegedly under the control of a 'philanthropic' United Nations, would have the power to save us from a whole variety of life and world-threatening disasters. A classic example would be the threat of an invasion from outer space. Have you noticed the increased hype in the media the past couple of years about people claiming to have been abducted and taken aboard alien spaceships?"

"Now that you mention it, especially on the TV talk shows," Scott agreed. "So what are you saying?"

"Well, people have done some digging. One of them is a guy named Bill Cooper. He wrote a book, *Behold a Pale Horse*. He says there are secret societies called the Illuminati, or the Illuminated Ones, who consider themselves the guardians of the 'Secrets of the Ages'.

"The most important of all is the Brotherhood of the Snake, or Dragon, and known as the Mysteries. The snake and dragon are symbols that represent wisdom. The father of wisdom is Lucifer, also called the Light Bearer. The focus of worship for the Mysteries was Osiris, another name of Lucifer. Osiris was the name of a bright star that the ancients believed had been cast down onto the earth. The literal meaning of Lucifer is 'bringer of light' or 'the morning star.'

"After Osiris was gone from the sky, the ancients saw the Sun as the representation of Osiris, or more correctly, Lucifer. These secret societies have different names, but their agenda is the same—they would abolish private property, religion, state sovereignty, and would reshape the social system of the world by taking control of individual countries, one by one, creating a New World Order."

"Sounds like Nazism or Communism," Carmen said.

"And a lot of other 'isms.' But the thing to keep in mind is that Illuminists have been discovered in both the Right and Left political camps. They may be members of the Christian or Jewish religions, but only to further their our goals. They want to gain complete control of the wealth, natural resources, and manpower of the whole world and they will eliminate Christians, Jews, and everyone else who won't sing their tune.

"One very important society is the Roshaniya. New members take an oath of allegiance only to the Order and swear that they will bind themselves to perpetual silence and unshaken loyalty and submission. Anyone who doesn't identify himself as a member is lawful prey.

"The secret sign is to pass a hand over the forehead, palm inward, the countersign, to hold the ear with the fingers and support the elbow in the other hand. With them, there is no Heaven, no hell, only a spirit state completely different from life as we know it."

"How many of the present world leaders do you think belong to a secret society?" Scott wanted to know.

"Most, according to Cooper and other investigators. That's how they get into positions of power. Did you know most of the judges in the country and a lot of lawyers are Masons? Call these groups what you will—for a long time they have all worked toward the same goal, the New World Order.

"Who are some of these societies?" Scott asked.

Lenny dug into the pages of his Bible and found a slip of paper. "I made a list one day from Cooper's book. Here listen to this: Order of the Quest, the Jason Society, the Roshaniya, the Qabbalah, the Knights Templar, the Knights of Malta, the Knights of Columbus, the Jesuits, the Masons, the Ancient and Mystical Order of Rosae Crucis, the Illuminati, the Nazi Party, the Communist Party, the Executive Members of the Council on Foreign Relations, The Group, the Brotherhood of the Dragon, the Rosicrucians, the Royal Institute of International Affairs, the Trilateral Commission, the Bilderberg Group, the Open Friendly Secret Society (the Vatican), the Russell Trust, the Skull & Bones, the Scroll & Key, the Order.

"There are more, but that will give you an idea. Evidently, many of them disagree on who will rule the New World Order, and that's why they sometimes pull in different directions. The Vatican, for instance, wants the Pope to head the world coalition. Some want Lord Maitreya to be head. Witnesses say he was present on the ship at Malta with Bush, Gorbachev and the ten regional heads of their future government.

"Keep in mind, also, that the rank and file of these societies are kept in the dark about the true motives of the top echelon. Take the Council on Foreign Relations, for instance. Many members—in fact, the majority—never serve on executive committees. They never go through any initiation. They are the power base and, in reality, are being used. The Executive Committee is the inner core of intimate associates, members of a secret society called the Order of the Quest, also known as the Jason Society. The rank and file are the outer circle on whom the inner core acts by personal persuasion, patronage and social pressure. That's how they bought Henry Kissinger. Rockefeller gave Kissinger a grant of $50,000 in the early '50's, a fortune in those days, and he became a member of the CFR. Anyone in the outer circle who doesn't toe the mark is expelled and the lesson is not lost on those who remain.

"The real power heads are men who are always recruited, without exception, from the secret societies of Harvard and Yale, known as the Skull & Bones and the Scroll & Key. Both societies are secret branches, also called the Brotherhood of Death, or what is otherwise historically known as the Illuminati. They are connected to parent organizations in Europe. There's a group at Oxford University, and one at the All Souls College in Germany, the Thule Society, also called the Brotherhood of Death.

"George Bush is a member of the Order. Surprised? You shouldn't be. Bush's father was also a member who helped finance Hitler.

"You've got to remember that the members of the Order take an oath that absolves them from any allegiance to any nation, or king, or government, or constitution, and that includes any subsequent oath they may have taken.

"Bill Cooper and other researchers believe that George Bush is not a loyal citizen of the United States but is loyal only to the goal of bringing the U.S. down to a third world country status and into the New World Order. According to the oath Bush took when he was initiated into the Skull & Bones, his oath of office as President meant nothing.

"Investigators have uncovered evidence that every branch of our government contains members of these groups who are conspiring to bring the United States down."

Scott had heard and read about this conspiracy before from patriot investigators but he had been skeptical, to say the least. But suddenly, he was struck with a thought. "You know, in order for the antichrist to take over the world that Revelation speaks about, a lot of preparation must be made. He's not going to do it over a weekend."

"Right on," Lenny agreed. "Now you got it. The way is being prepared as we speak. These societies have always had the same agenda and the elite at the very top have always been into some form of Satan worship. They were held at bay, so to speak, through the ages by God, until *His* agenda is completed—which it almost is, apparently."

"Okay," Carmen cut in, "so why sweat it? God's got it all worked out."

"Oh yeah?" Lenny snapped back. "We Christians got a job to do, right up to the end. Our prayers, backed by our actions, keep the enemy out of the camp until God is ready."

"Action meaning picking up guns, right?" Carmen demanded.

Lenny half smiled. "Now, how did I know you'd say that?" Then his smile faded. "I believe there are Christians who could be used of the Lord in that way, but they better be convinced by the lord, and not by the mob mentality of a town meeting.

"Who exactly are the Bilderbergers?" Scott asked.

"They are perhaps the most powerful secret organization in the world. They were organized in 1952 and named after the hotel where the first meeting took place in 1954. The man who organized the Bilderberg Group, Prince Bernhard of the Netherlands, has the power to veto the Vatican's choice of any Pope it selects. The Prince has this veto power because his family, the Hapsburgs, are descended from the Roman emperors.

"The core of the organization consists of three committees, made up of thirteen members each. The heart of the Bilderberg Group consists of 39 total members. The three committees are exclusively members of all the different secret groups that make up the Illuminati, the Freemasons, the Vatican, and the Black Nobility.

"This committee works year round in offices in Switzerland. It determines who is invited to the annual meeting and what policies and plans will be discussed. This very secretive and elite group is directing the 'quiet war' against us."

"You never hear about them in the media," Scott offered.

"Precisely. What does that tell you? The very fact that a meeting is secret and never reported tells me that something is going on that I would not approve. Don't ever believe that grown men meet on a regular basis just to put on fancy robes, hold candles, and glad-hand each other. These men meet for important reasons and their meetings are secret because the community wouldn't approve."

"But how can so few men hope to bring all this about?" Carmen asked.

"Simple. They control corrupt politicians and the bankers. The bankers control the money flow to the countries, through commerce, wars, even narcotics.

"One brain child of theirs is the Trilateral Commission which is an elite group of some 300 very prominent business, political, and intellectual decision-makers of Western Europe, North America and Japan. This enterprise is a private agency that works to build up political and economic cooperation among the three regions. Its grand design, which it no longer hides, is the New World Order.

"The Trilateral Commission was the idea of its founder, American banking magnate, David Rockefeller. The real reason for its formation was the decline of the Council on Foreign Relation's power, as a result of the peoples' dissatisfaction with the Vietnam War. Its goal is the consolidation of all commercial and banking interests, by controlling the political government of the United States."

"Okay, let's say all this is true," Scott said, "though I'm still not totally convinced. But, even if it's only ten percent true, shouldn't we be shouting it from the house tops, warning everyone?"

Lenny shrugged. "No argument there. Trouble is, most people won't believe you. I quit beating my head against the wall a long time ago. Every so often you'll find an eager soul God seems to have prepared and you save your breath for him.

"As for your own search for the truth, Scott, a very wise man said one time, 'listen to everything, look at everything, think it over, and then make your decision. But until you've done that, until you've given all the evidence an honest look, don't rush to judgment.' Most people do that, you know."

"Sounds like good advice," Scott agreed.

Lenny rubbed his forehead in thought. "Tell you what. I got a book with me I'll let you read that will give you some hard facts."

Before they retired that evening, Lenny handed Scott a book entitled, *Operation Vampire Killer 2000* published by "Police Against the New World Order."

Using a borrowed flashlight, Scott read that night from the book by Jack McLamb, the most decorated Phoenix, Arizona, police officer in history.

The opening paragraph read, "The police officers, National Guardsmen, and military officers who have contributed to this special publication are aware of a plan to overthrow the Constitutional Republic of these United States of America.

"Let it be well understood, that we, protectors of the American People, have not asked for this battle. It is our nation's enemies who have brought this fight to the very door of every good American. Be it resolved: our prayer and promise is to do all within our power, as faithful countrymen, to overthrow this evil, treasonous plan in a completely non-violent, lawful manner.

"Our sworn duty is to protect the people of this nation and its constitution, and republican form of government from any enemy that would come against it. Our pledge is that we will, by every means given unto us, uphold our oaths and fulfill our sworn duty to our countrymen."

Scott was moved by the pledge. Next, McLamb offered quotes from famous people.

"'The great rule of conduct for us, in regard to foreign nations, is in extending our commercial relations to have as little political connection as possible...it is our true policy to steer clear of permanent alliances with any portion of the foreign world.'" George Washington, Sept. 19, 1796.

"Senator Hoagland, state senator from Nebraska in 1983, said over radio, 'Fundamental, Bible believing people do not have the right to indoctrinate their children in their religions beliefs because we, the State, are preparing them for the year 2000, when America will be part of a one-world global society, and their children will not fit in.'"

Scott could hardly believe what he had just read. He lay there for a long time looking at the page and a tinge of resentment and fear flitted through him. He read on.

"David Rockefeller, internationalist billionaire humanist, CFR kingpin, founder of the Trilateral Commission, World Order Godfather, and in all probability, the high school graduate voted most-likely-to-be-hanged-for-treason, voiced his praise of the controlled U.S. media for keeping their oath not to divulge the globalist plans to the public.

"Speaking to his fellow conspirators at a Bilderberger meeting in June, 1991, in Baden, Germany. Mr. Rockefeller stated, 'We are grateful to the *Washington Post*, the *New York Times*, *Time Magazine,* and other great publications whose directors have attended our meetings and respected their promises of discretion for almost forty years...it would have been impossible for us to develop our plan for the world if we had been subject to the bright lights of publicity during those years. But the world is now more sophisticated and prepared to march towards a world government. The supranational sovereignty of an intellectual elite and world bankers is surely preferable to the national autodetermination practiced in past centuries.'"

Scott couldn't believe that the media had been deliberately silent about this conspiracy. Rockefeller's statement was mind-boggling. Reading rapidly now, he came to the chapter, "Media Blacks Out The Facts." He read that John Swinton, former chief of staff of the *New York Times*, gave a toast before the New York Press Club.

He said, "There is no such thing, at this date of the world's history, in America, as an independent press. You know it and I know it. There is not one of you who dares to write your honest opinions, and if you did, you know beforehand that it would never appear in print.

"I am paid weekly for keeping my honest opinion out of the paper I am connected with. Others of you are paid similar salaries for similar things, and any of you who would be so foolish as to write honest opinions would be out on the street looking for another job. If I allowed my honest opinions to appear in one issue of my paper, before twenty-four hours, my occupation would he gone.

"The business of the journalist is to destroy the truth, to lie outright, to pervert, to vilify, to fawn at the feet of mammon, and to sell his country and his race for his daily bread. You know it and I know it and what folly is this toasting an independent press? We are the tools and vassals of rich men behind the scenes. We are the jumping jacks, they pull the strings and we dance. Our talents, our possibilities and our lives are all the property of other men. We are intellectual prostitutes."

Scott put the book down and reflected about some of the recent news reported in the media. Most of it had supported the government's agenda, or the large corporations, or dwelled on crime, *ad nauseam*. While the congress ramrodded G.A.T.T. through, the media seemed innocently distracted by the daily skirmishes of the O.J. Simpson trial. Another piece of the puzzle had slipped into place for him. He returned to the book.

"Richard M. Cohan, senior producer of CBS political news, said: 'We are going to impose our agenda on the (news) coverage by dealing with issues and subjects that *we* choose to deal with.'

"Richard Salant, former president of CBS News, stated: 'Our job is to give people not what they want, but what *we* decide they ought to have.'

"Norman Thomas, for many years the U.S. socialist

presidential candidate, proclaimed: 'The American people will not ever knowingly adopt socialism. But under the name of "liberalism' they will adopt every fragment of the socialist program, until one day, America will be a socialist nation, without knowing how it happened.'

"Walter Cronkite: 'News reporters are certainly liberal (socialists) and left of center.'

"Barbara Walters: 'The news media in general are liberals (socialists).'"

But what Scott read next really shocked him.

"David Spangler, director of Planetary Initiative—a United Nations World government group—stated: 'No one will enter the New World Order unless he or she will make a pledge to worship Lucifer. No one will enter the New Age unless he will take a luciferian initiation.'"

Then Scott read a quote from Ralph Nader: "Is there a number or mark planned for the hand or forehead in a new cashless society? Yes, and I have seen the machines that are now ready to put it into operation."

Scott was sure the "mark" had to be the mark of the beast, servant to Lucifer, mentioned in Revelation 13. "...And that no man might buy or sell save he that had the mark, or the name of the beast, or the number of his name (666)."

He closed the book and let out a big sigh. He was no longer a skeptic. There was just too much evidence from too many sources. He needed to get to a roof top. But which roof top, and when?

SIX

Scott didn't mean to oversleep. He and Carmen were being released at 10:00 that morning and he wanted to glean the last bit of information he could from Lenny. But he had read a long time and then stayed awake trying to develop some sort of plan of action for his family and the Maranatha people.

After he packed the few things Amy had brought him, he and Carmen sat down with Lenny for their farewells.

"Lenny, it's been great. You've helped me see some things," Scott said.

"Yes, thanks for everything." Carmen concurred.

"Just remember me once in awhile when you're talking to the Lord," Lenny said.

"You know we will," Scott answered.

"Especially that you get a fair shake from the judge and you can have Jennifer back," Carmen added.

Lenny bowed his head and when he looked up his eyes were soft. "She's the reason I got started with this stuff, you know. Man, how I miss that kid." He took a deep breath. "But some day we'll know why we have to go through this crap. I know one thing, I'm a lot smarter about the system because of her. Sometimes we have to be slapped good and hard to wake us up. Stay informed, guys, listen to your short-wave. You won't get the truth from the networks. Listen to Valentine, Bill Cooper, Norm Resnick; they all approach the problem differently. Remember the frequencies I gave you—12.165 during the day, 5.065, at night."

"How much time do we have before things start falling apart?" Scott asked.

"Our economy could collapse any time, it's a house built of cards, which means, you could easily have food lines and rioting. It wouldn't take a whole lot for the government to declare martial law, especially if the militia fights back when the Feds come after our guns. I read in the *Spotlight* that Reno has sent notices to her D.A.s' in the states to start surveillance on all patriot groups. She's said in public that militia groups are terrorists. That's the crap they'll feed the press when they begin to move full scale."

"How can they possibly hope to confiscate all our guns?" Carmen asked. "The NRA claims there are at least 90 million gun owners in the country."

"Well, what they did in other countries was to first con the citizens to turn their weapons in. The hype goes something like this: do your part to lessen the chance of criminals getting guns, turn your weapon in as your patriotic duty, and to even make it painless for you, we'll pay you to do it. And, of course, the funds will come from our own tax dollars.

"They know most citizens will fall for this because we are self-indulged and preoccupied with making enough money to get by in a drowning economy, and are brainwashed by the media. What they are definitely paranoid about are the guys who would rather be dead than slaves—the militia."

"So, is that how the United Nations troops get involved, I read about in your book?"

"Right. The patriots have grown too powerful, too

soon. The masses will follow a line of least resistance or what's self-serving. Just give them their Sunday football, a 6-pack, a weekly check and you own them. They say you could get Vodka cheap in Russia during the hardest times."

"So now you've got, what, maybe 50,000 militia, at most, facing down how many foreign troops?" Scott asked.

"No one knows exactly; the Pentagon doesn't talk much. They put out this jive that in '92, Bush invited United Nations troops to train here, that it's all legal. Now, there could be from 20 to 60,000 here. One thing's for sure, they've brought in tons of Russian armament. Trains of over 100 cars with Russian tanks and armored personnel carriers have been sighted by patriots, one I remember was at Altoona, Pennsylvania."

Scott had been away from his short-wave for more than six months, but he remembered the stories of sightings of black unmarked helicopters buzzing patriots' homes, especially in Florida. They flew mostly at night, very low, with gun doors open and machine guns plainly visible. Ex-army guys who would know said some of them were Soviet M1-8 HIP machines.

"Ever hear of a guy called Mark from Michigan?" Lenny asked. Neither Scott or Carmen had.

"He's getting big on short-wave. I guess he was in the intelligence in the service. According to him, there are three groups of military and police forces. The first group is the multi-jurisdictional task force—the national guard, ATF, FBI, local and state police, and a national police force. The next level up are called Fincen troops—foreign military and secret police brought into the U.S. for deployment against U.S. citizens. At the highest level, supposedly, are United Nations battle groups. They have been entering the U.S. by orders Bush signed and are training here to control Americans during the implementation of FEMA, the Federal Emergency Management Agency. They will run things when Martial law is declared. When you consider all this, it makes a lot of sense to start preparing."

"How do you prepare?" Scott asked.

"I know what I intend to do," Carmen said. "I'm going to be looking for a militia unit to tie up with."

"That's the part I've still got a real problem with," Scott said. "I don't see Jesus telling his disciples to pick up arms against the Roman government."

"Are you aware, my friend," Lenny said solemnly, that many of the freedom fighters during the Revolutionary War were Christians, that quite a few ministers either supported them, or became fighters, themselves?"

"I've heard that, but it doesn't necessarily prove a case for a Christian to pick up a gun."

"Hey, guy," Carmen said, "if they hadn't, America wouldn't even be here today."

"I'm not so sure," Scott said.

"Wait a minute," Lenny said. "What are you driving at?"

Scott thought a minute. "Well, how do we know that God didn't have a better plan for the birth of America than what happened? Maybe all that bloodletting could have been avoided."

Carmen shook his head in disbelief. Lenny rubbed his ear, his face twisted in thought.

"It seems," Scott continued, "the Christians who want to fight the government hang their arguments on one or two verses in Scripture, where the disciples tell Jesus they have two swords and He says 'that is enough.' That's all He says. He doesn't tell them to get more, or to resist, and what He meant exactly is a puzzle, but it would be stupid to try to make Jesus an armed rebel. His whole message was to love your enemies, turn the other cheek, don't retaliate when persecuted, do good to them who use you. As for the government, when's the last time you read Romans 13?"

He pulled out a pocket Bible. "Here, listen to this, 'Let every soul be subject unto the higher powers. For there is no power but of God: the powers that be are ordained of God. Whosoever therefore resists the power, resists the ordinance of God, and they that resist shall receive to themselves damnation.'

"The way I see it, every government in the history of man came to power because God allowed it, even evil governments. He used them to chastise Israel more than once in the Old Testament. He allowed the evil Roman government and Pontius Pilate to crucify Christ, and if Christ hadn't submitted, you and I, brothers, would be on our way to a very hot place because there wouldn't be anyone around to save us."

"I don't know, man." Carmen looked very skeptical.

Lenny was still thoughtful. "Is it possible God could lead some men to be pacifists, like Ghandi or King, and at the same time, lead others to put up armed resistance?"

"Well, I guess He could," Scott answered.

"I believe there's enough Scripture to support resisting evil whenever we find it," Lenny said. "For instance, Ephesians 5:11 says we should reprove the works of darkness."

"No argument," Scott concurred. "We're suppose to take a stand, but King's civil disobedience is a far cry from shooting an ATF guy who wants your gun."

Carmen was disgusted. "Man, what are you talking

about? Sometimes you give me heartburn. You've heard the plan; first they take your gun, then they can do pretty much what they want. What about your wife and kids? You going to sit there and tell me you wouldn't defend them with a gun if you had to?"

Scott didn't answer. He could throw out a smart comeback, but his honesty wouldn't allow it. The question was puzzling. Did the Scriptures allow a man to pick up arms to defend his family? If one took Jesus's teachings literally, which he thought he did, then the answer was "no." And what of the Old Testament, where God told His people to arm themselves and resist to the last man, if need be? Did he not have a right to defend Amy and the kids?

He was supposed to walk in faith because without faith it was impossible to please God, he knew the verses well. When the crisis came, was he just to call on Jesus to miraculously save his family from harm? Could he expect to be spared tribulation because he was a Christian? Then what of the martyrs? He knew that every one of the apostles except John had been killed, many in very cruel ways.

He remembered reading a book, *Fox's Book of Martyrs*, about an army, a Roman legion of 6,600 men, who had all become Christians. The emperor ordered one man in every ten killed if they did not denounce Christ. Eventually, they were all sacrificed, every last one. What struck Scott was that they were trained to fight, highly skilled combatants, who might possibly have slashed their way to freedom. But to a man, they chose to sacrifice their lives instead.

Carmen was watching him closely, waiting for an answer. He knew Carmen looked to him for strength, sometimes too much so, rather than seeking God.

"You want to know the truth? I honestly don't know

what I'll do."

Carmen didn't like his answer. Lenny sat back in his chair and took a deep breath. "Somehow that doesn't sound like the kinda thing a man who would chain himself to a cross would say."

Scott felt a little foolish but he had nothing more. A guard appeared and called their names. "Well, that's it," Lenny said. "I'll give you a call sometime. Let's keep in touch. If you lose my address or number, just call the DuPage county sheriff's office, they know us well." He gave them both a bear hug and escorted them to the side gate the guard was opening for them.

And then they were out in the parking lot and Amy was running toward him, her embrace and the kids hugging his neck—the most wonderful feeling in the world!

SEVEN

So Scott returned to his two room apartment on Chicago's near north side, and to his cab driving and the Maranatha meetings which had grown both in size and fervor while he was away.

It seemed that what he had been preaching to them all along, that the group shouldn't expect him, or one or two others, to be the "life of the party" when they gathered together, but to expect God to use each of them to participate with the gifts and talents He gives to every believer, was now bearing fruit.

For months, he had quoted I Corin. 14:26 "How is it then brethren? When you come together, every one of you has a psalm, a doctrine, a tongue, a revelation, an interpretation. Let all things be done unto edifying...if anything be revealed to another that sits by, let the first one hold his peace. For you may all prophesy one by one, that all may learn, and all may be comforted."

From the very beginning of their meetings, Scott's goal had been to worship God in spirit and truth, to learn from God's word what He expected from His people, and to meet the needs of the people present. How often in earlier days, had he sat disappointed in dry denominational church services because his spiritual needs had not been met?

He struggled with this problem much, thinking he

was to blame. But when Amy expressed the same dissatisfaction, he felt relieved. The Pentecostals came closest to hitting the mark. But though they replaced the Baptists' dry lectures with flamboyant preachers and high emotionalism, they, too, missed it, in his judgment.

What he yearned for was a service where one could express a burden or a joy, at will, where one wouldn't feel lonely and unimportant, or that the service would be exactly the same, whether one attended or not.

As he laboriously studied the Scriptures to discover where the modern church had gone wrong, he saw that in the early assemblies, God was the audience and the worshippers were the performers. But in modern denominational services, the pastor was the performer, and the worshippers, the audience. Fellowship was confined to the foyer afterward. Try to speak, and the ushers would "ush" you out. But he discovered the New Testament church almost demanded individual participation when it met.

From other books about early church history, he learned that the Roman empire, realizing it could not eliminate Christianity after martyring thousands of believers, adopted it in the third century. One of the most seemingly harmless, but devastatingly effective changes was the replacement of Scriptural worship by providing a building where large numbers of people would congregate, sitting row behind row, as spectators. The daily corporate breaking of bread from house to house and spontaneous interaction was not encouraged and gradually ceased.

The openness and willingness to exchange with one another, to build one another up, was painfully absent, replaced by Rome's system of "church," the "celebration" of the mass.

But one of the most significant facts he was to discover was, that though Martin Luther and other reformation fathers recognized the correct basis of salvation, the importance of Scripture, and the many unscriptural doctrines of Rome like: the "sacrifice" of the mass, Mariolatry, worship of saints, or purgatory, they seemingly missed a very important truth. Had they modeled their meetings after the New Testament Church, the body of Christ would have experienced restoration instead of reformation. Evidently, they did not recognize how vital personal involvement was by each believer.

Though they removed the altar, and did away with practically all the "do-it-yourself" salvation gimmicks, and preached doctrine in the assemblies, they apparently believed it the most important activity needed to develop spiritual maturity.

That this practice was not enough, was demonstrated by the lukewarmness and ineffectiveness of the present day Protestant church, Scott concluded. In a day when a former God-fearing nation had turned to many forms of idol worship—where immorality was sky-rocketing—the great body of believers who were supposed to be the salt of the earth, who, it was once said of their spiritual ancestors that they turned the world upside down, was still practicing a twice removed form of Romish tradition. It had a form of Godliness but denied the power, and was sadly ineffective in producing dynamic believers who could influence their lost neighbors.

So through a lot of teaching and exhortation, Scott could finally boast that the Maranatha meetings were now all he had ever hoped for—with wholesale participation and great expectation that Jesus would show up at every service.

He wondered if he could ever go it alone without them. The uneasiness about the country's future he had experienced in jail lingered on, and to stay informed, he hovered over his short-wave in the evenings.

Things were definitely heating up, especially in the south. Some counties in Florida had served notice that if the B.A.T.F. crossed their borders looking for guns, they would resist on constitutional grounds. The militia was rapidly expanding across the states, Michigan boasted a conservative 14,000; single counties in Florida, alone, claimed 4,000. Surprisingly, Tom Brokaw and Donahue both did segments on the militia.

Tom Valentine interviewed Michael Benn on his show. Benn, who had collected twelve million signatures to impeach President Clinton, was awakened early one morning to the sound of black helicopters flying very low over his neighborhood. On the second pass, the neighbor's home across the street was engulfed in flames. Neighbors reported hearing a loud roar and seeing rockets being fired at the home's roof. Benn believed the attackers targeted the wrong house.

Bob Fletcher with the Militia of Montana appeared as a guest on several short-wave shows. He was warning the people that the nation was headed for a massive economic collapse, engineered by an element in government. Supposedly, after the collapse food riots would break out, allowing the government to impose martial law and the confiscation of firearms.

He reported that the Pentagon had a project to sell military bases to foreign governments, one being an air force base in Texas, sold to the Germans. Fletcher claimed his research had uncovered that the wealthy elite, the international bankers and their associates, had prepared luxurious shelters in Australia and the Far East to survive world chaos and nuclear war.

Nuclear war? The very thought gave Scott the sweats. Would God deal that harshly with America? His mind raced to chapters in Revelation where one-third of the world's population was destroyed with fire. Then one night on short-wave, he heard of a book by a Romanian Bible smuggler, Dumitru Dudaman, who had received a visit from a heavenly being who forecasted America's future. When the book arrived, Scott stayed up all night and read it through.

Dudaman had been tortured and imprisoned by the Romanian police, and while in jail, had a visitation from an angel who told him he would be released and would then go to America. He was released, miraculously, and when he was in America a few months, he received another visit.

Dudaman wrote: "Late one night I could not sleep. The children were sleeping on the luggage. My wife and daughter were crying. I went outside and walked around. I didn't want them to see me cry. I walked around the building, crying and saying, 'God! Why did you punish me? Why did you bring me into this country? I can't understand anybody. If I try to ask anybody anything, all I hear is, 'I don't know.'

"I stopped in front of the apartment and sat on a large rock. Suddenly a bright light came toward me. I jumped to my feet because it looked as if a car was coming directly at me, attempting to run me down. I thought the Romanian secret police had tracked me to America, and now they were trying to kill me. But it wasn't a car at all. As the light approached, it surrounded me. From the light I heard the same voice that I had heard so many times in prison. He asked, 'Dumitru, why are you so despaired?'

"I asked, 'Why did you punish me? Why did you bring me to this country? I have nowhere to lay my head down. I can't understand anybody.'

'Dumitru, didn't I tell you I am here with you also? I brought you to this country because this country will burn.'

"I asked, 'Then why did you bring me here to burn? Why didn't you let me die in my own country? You should have let me die in jail in Romania!'

"He said, 'Dumitru, have patience so I can tell you. Get on this.' I got on something next to him. I don't know what it was. I also know that I was not asleep. It was not a dream. It was not a vision. I was awake, just as I am now.

"He showed me all of California and said, 'This is Sodom and Gomorrah. All of this, in one day, it will burn! It's sin has reached the Holy One.' Then he took me to Las Vegas. 'This is Sodom and Gomorrah. In one day it will burn.' Then he showed me the state of New York. 'Do you know what this is?' he asked.

"I said, 'No.'

"He said, 'This is New York. This is Sodom and Gomorrah! In one day, it will burn.'

"Then he showed me all of Florida. 'This is Florida,' he said. 'This is Sodom and Gomorrah. In one day, it will burn.'

"Then he took me back home to the rock where we had begun. 'All of this I have shown you—in one day, it will burn! '

"I asked, 'How will it burn?'

"He said, 'Remember what I am telling you, because you will go on television, on the radio, and to churches. You must yell with a loud voice. Do not be afraid, because I will be with you.'

"I asked, 'How will I be able to go? Who knows me here in America? I don't know anybody here.'

"He said, 'Don't worry yourself. I will go before

you. I will do a lot of healing in the American churches, and I will open the doors for you. But do not say anything else besides what I tell you. This country will burn.'

"I asked, 'What will you do with the Church?'

"He said, 'I want to save the Church, but the churches have forsaken me.'

"I asked, 'How did they forsake you?'

"He said, 'The people praise themselves. The honor that the people are supposed to give Jesus Christ, they take upon themselves. In the churches there are divorces. There is adultery in the churches. There are homosexuals in the churches. There is abortion in the churches, and all other sins that are possible. Because of the sin, I have left some of the churches. You must yell in a loud voice that they must put an end to their sinning. They must turn toward the Lord. The Lord never gets tired of forgiving. They must draw close to the Lord and live a clean life. If they have sinned until now, they must put an end to it, and start a new life, as the Bible tells them to live.'

"'How will America burn?' I asked. 'America is the most powerful country in this world. Why did you bring us here to burn? Why didn't you, at least, let us die where all the Dudumans have died?'

"He said, 'Remember this, Dumitru. The Russian spies have discovered where the nuclear warehouses are in America. When the Americans will think there is peace and safety, from the middle of the country, some of the people will start fighting against the government. The government will be busy with internal problems. Then from the ocean, from Cuba, Nicaragua, Mexico...' (He told me two other countries, but I didn't remember what they were)...they will bomb the nuclear warehouses. When they explode, America will

77

burn!'

"'What will you do with the Church of the Lord? How will you save the ones that will turn toward you?' I asked.

"He said, 'Tell them this: how I saved the three young ones from the furnace of fire, and how I saved Daniel in the lions' den, is the same way I will save them.'"

The angel went on to tell Dudaman that America was the mystery Babylon mentioned in Revelation. "...because all the nations of the world immigrated to America with their own gods and were not stopped. Encouraged by the freedom here, the wickedness began to increase. Later on, even though America was established as a Christian nation, the American people began to follow the strange gods that the immigrants had brought in, and also turned their backs on the God who had built and prospered this country."

With only an hour's sleep, but jacked up with a lot of coffee, Scott somehow made it through the next day. But when he had to endure long waiting in cab lines between fares, his mind would return to Dudaman's warnings. These were serious words and he believed they were from God. A part of him did not want to believe that God would ever allow nuclear war to come to America, but the country had changed drastically in a few short years.

Old cherished moral codes were thrown away in every aspect of life—the courts had legalized the murder of more than a million infants a year. Most Americans, claiming to believe in God, bowed down daily to the gods of drugs, alcohol, sex and materialism.

Most denominational churches had become little more than social clubs, whose pastors gave lectures that were more entertaining than convicting, were more concerned about their jobs than the eternal destiny of their flocks. He remembered, too, that America was the only country to have killed thousands of civilians with a nuclear bomb. Was it now her turn? At any rate, if God didn't deal with America, he reflected, then He certainly owed Sodom and Gomorrah an apology.

What he found interesting was the angel's words that Russia would attack when America had internal problems in the middle of the country. Scott knew the militia was most active in the midwestern states.

Fear began to gnaw at him. Praying helped some, but an oppressive spirit continued to harass him. His guilt grew, too, for he knew the Scriptures well, that he must live by faith and trust in God.

In his Bible study he tried to take solace from Jesus's words, in Matthew 6:25-34. "Therefore I say unto you, take no thought for your life, what you shall eat, or what you shall drink; nor yet for your body, what you shall put on. Is not the life more than meat, and the body than raiment? Behold the fowls of the air: for they sow not, neither do they reap, nor gather into barns; yet your heavenly Father feedeth them. Are you not much better than they.

"Which of you by taking thought can add one cubit unto his stature? And why take you thought for raiment? Consider the lilies of the field, how they grow; they toil not, neither do they spin: And yet I say unto you, that even Solomon in all his glory was not arrayed like one of these. Wherefore, if God so clothe the grass of the field, which today is, and tomorrow is cast into the oven, shall he not much more clothe you, oh ye of little faith?

"Therefore take no thought, saying, 'What shall we eat?' or, 'What shall we drink' or, 'Wherewithal shall we be clothed?' (For after all these things do the Gentiles seek:) for your heavenly Father knoweth that you have need of all these things. But seek ye first the kingdom of God, and his righteousness; and all these things shall be added unto you.

"Take therefore, no thought for the morrow: for the morrow shall take thought for the things of itself. Sufficient unto the day is the evil thereof."

After much meditation, Scott finally determined that he would not let himself become a spiritual "yo-yo," moved by daily short-wave reports that were discouraging and fed his fears, so he decided to "notch" out their signals, at least for awhile. Except for one with the graveled voice—the one who demanded and got Scott's utmost attention—Brother Stair.

EIGHT

"Get out of the cities, Brothers and Sisters," Preacher Stair was screaming daily to America. "The cities are about to go up in smoke, food will become scarce, the largest supermarkets only have a week's supply on their shelves. There will be rioting. Jesus Christ is coming soon! Prepare to meet your God!"

Stair called himself a "last day prophet of God" and was convinced he was preaching to the last generation. But though he had a short fuse with callers-in to his talk show who didn't totally agree with him, Scott had to admit Stair was definitely a lone voice crying in the wilderness. No other preacher on radio or television consistently beat the drum as loud as he.

Stair was convinced the patriots were working against God, that the New World Order was devised by God to allow the antichrist of Revelation to rise to power, and insist that everyone take his mark in order to buy or sell.

Scott knew the verse in Revelation 13 well. "And he caused all, both small and great, rich and poor, free and bond, to receive a mark in their right hand, or in their foreheads, and that no man might buy or sell, save he that had the mark, or the name of the beast, or the number of his name. Here is wisdom. Let him that

81

has understanding count the number of the beast, for it is the number of a man and his number is six hundred threescore and six (666)."

Scott had first heard of the antichrist and his 666 number from fellow students in high school who claimed to have joined the occult and defaced Christians' lockers with the number and the satanic star.

Ralph Nader's shocking statement in Lenny's book was still indeed on the "back burner" of his mind—"is there a number or mark planned for the hand or forehead in a new cashless society? Yes, and I have seen the machines that are now ready to put it into operation." So when he happened across a conversation one night on his radio between Lou Epton and Terry Cook on the subject, it got his full attention.

Epton: It's good to have you, Terry. You have some interesting information, but before we really get into it, tell us about your background.

Cook: Okay. I'm 45 years old. I'm a retired Los Angeles deputy sheriff and a former state fraud investigator for the State of California. A few years ago, I discovered there was a plan to take the globe cashless by international bankers. They have a plan that will ultimately lead to a form of enslavement by means of computers, whereby a computer chip will be installed under our skins and will be the means by which we do our buying and selling.

Epton: Terry, do you think people will just voluntarily allow the bureaucrats to do this?

Cook: Well, no. They're going to coerce us into doing it. We are being conditioned into it by having our pets injected with identifying micro-computer chips at the present time.

Epton: I remember seeing literature in this regard where they packaged it very nicely, saying, you'll always know where your pet is. We transformed some of the words as we read through the brochure from this particular pet supplier. You could easily change the word "pet" to "child." But you really feel there is an over-all plan to inject Americans?

Cook: Absolutely. One of the arguments for it is that our current system is very susceptible to fraud. Stolen cards or numbers have caused loses in the millions. A better method, they say, would be to insert a bio-chip, uniquely yours, under the skin of your hand or just at the edge of the hairline of your forehead. It will be the most perfect method of financial transactions anyone has ever devised. Convenience is the buzz word, of course. You just go to the store, pass your hand over the scanner, and your account is debited. Not a dime passes hands.

Epton: It certainly looks as though we're headed toward a cashless society. They've got, now, what they call a smart card, just like Master or Visa credit cards, you carry it instead of cash.

Cook: Right. In fact, the smart card, Lou, will carry up to six billion bytes of information. Virtually your entire life's history can be programmed into a little tiny wafer chip. That, in itself, is scary enough. We will be totally at the whim and call of the New World Order crowd.

Epton: What got you on this track, Terry?

Cook: Well, for most of my life, like a lot of people, I just wandered around in our society, wondering what was going on. In 1983, I became acquainted with a Christian who told me 'You know, if I am reading Scripture right, it looks as though this may be the final generation that the Bible said would occur at the end of the age.' And, of course, the end of the age is the year 2000. That sparked my interest. I was basically an agnostic. I hadn't really decided one way or the other.

So I began investigating, and indeed, it really amazed me just how coincidental, if you will, everything in the world that's happening seems to match up with prophecies in the Bible. I became a Christian and then a very intense investigator. For example, Lou, in Revelation 13, just before the end of the age, there will be a man called the antichrist who will come to power. This man will lead a global government of ten regional governments, world-wide, and will enslave the world. It says he will specifically cause them to take his mark in order to buy or sell. Now, think about that for a moment. In all of world history, this is the first time that a society can be enslaved by electronic wizardry. Is it coincidental that it's happening right at the end of the age?

I have studied this vigorously for the past few years. I have read 263 books by very reliable men. As a former investigator, I really screen my material carefully. Bill Clinton was educated, as he espouses, by the Rhodes scholarship program. Mr. Rhodes was a member of the Illuminati. As you know, Bill Clinton's a member of the Trilaterial Commission, the Council on Foreign Relation, and the International Bankers G-7 group, called the Bilderbergers. He was groomed from early on to be who he is today. And of course, George Bush gracefully stepped down. It was planned, and it is my opinion, that George Bush is not out of the picture yet, that soon, he will become the leader of the U.N.

Epton: I really had the feeling that they didn't really plan for Clinton to win, that they figured Bush would get back in. Even when they stuck in Ross Perot.

Cook: Well, Ross Perot is one of them, too, my friend.

Epton: I know that.

Cook: But anyway, Lou, very few people caught this. The day after the inauguration, in the *L.A. Times*, on the front page, the lead read "Clinton must now choose between big gambles, and or, safe bets.' And in the very first paragraph he says, 'we are now about to embark on the Novus Ordo Seclorum.'

Novus Ordo Seclorum is Latin and is on the back of the dollar bill. Look at the pyramid. It means New World Order. And in the next paragraph of this article it says that President Clinton, like many of his predecessors, invoked the spirit of the Novus Ordo Seclorum as he stood to deliver his inaugural address. But it's not Clinton's plan, it's the internationalists', the Illuminati.

Epton: An interesting thing, we had a Mr. G.S. Oden with us yesterday, who recently returned from Europe where he has considerable influence. He had a meeting at the Bank of Rothchild with some of their top people. His opening comment to me was, 'for a long, long time, Lou, I thought you were just really off the wall, but now that things have started to happen, I am finding out that you really have been on target.' He said, 'Do you know that the executives of the Bank of Rothchild admitted to me that, yes, they did finance both sides of the last two wars.'

Cook: Most people don't know that, Lou, and if you tell them, they'll laugh and scoff at you or look at you as if you were crazy. Americans, probably more than any other society, tend not to want to deal with reality, and I think a lot of it is caused by television. We have been tuned out of reality by means of the 'sickcom.' That's what I call the sitcoms. We are desensitized and lethargic. And I believe that's part of their brainwashing program so that they can gradually take us over and enslave us.

Epton: I can't argue that. But I wanted to get back to how the bio-chip implant works.

Cook: Okay. Most people, of course, are familiar with the bar coding system in stores, the UPC, universal product code. That system works by laser light. When you pass the bar code on the product over the laser light, it reads the spacing between the black bars and derives a numerical value from it. But if you cover the bar code, you can interrupt the measuring system and defeat it. Well, that's why radio frequency identification was invented. It can penetrate solid objects. All electromagnetic energy that we are aware of today is on a different frequency. Light is electromagnetic energy on a different frequency.

The system that uses it can't be defected or altered, and up until 1988, didn't even exist. About that time engineers at the Destron Corporation, in Boulder, Colorado, under the leadership of Dr. Carl Sanders, invented the bio-chip for human use. Sanders was an agnostic. When he developed this program he was witnessed to by a Christian, and the Christian told him, 'Hey, that looks like Revelation 13, my friend.' Sanders said he did some research, became a Christian, and now goes all over the world telling everybody about this demonic system he invented.

Epton: Interesting to note, too, that in the bar code if you follow this you will always find the 666.

Cook: Exactly, Lou. The entire UPC system has been invented and programmed around the number of the antichrist the Bible tells us will be existent in the last days.

Epton: Okay. Let's take some calls. Thanks for your patience. You're on the air.

Caller: Considering the system coming, how long

do you think it will be before checks are obsolete?

Cook: Yes, Ma'am. The best I've been able to estimate, Ma'am, is that in two or three years we will have been taken totally cashless, and this micro-chip implant program of identification will have been imposed around the globe. You see, they're planning a global economic stock market crash and an economic collapse, worldwide. Of course, this will create an emergency, and that's when they plan to impose this cashless system. Have you noticed, over the last three years how our economy has deteriorated? It's no accident, and it's going to get continually worse.

Caller: What do you think that will do to the price of gold and silver?

Cook: Well, eventually, it'll be eliminated as a means of financial transaction because if you do have a form of commodity outside of their system, that'll give you freedom. But, initially, we'll be able to use it to circumvent the system. We'll have an underground economy of bartering, if you will. But believe me, they will eventually pass laws against hoarding food and commodities such as gold and silver.

Caller: I want to ask one more question. How are they going to do search and seizure? Based on what. How will they confiscate property?

Cook: It will begin with financial collapse, or some catastrophic event, perhaps a national or international emergency that will allow them to say, 'Oh, gee, this is all terrible, isn't it? We need to suspend the Constitution and impose martial law.' And, it will not only be in the U.S. but it will be taken global. Remember, when you're under martial law you have no rights under the Constitution. You have no habeas corpus. You have no means by which you can protest. You're simply enslaved. That's the plan and it's very, very involved. It would take me a long time to really explain it.

You know, Lou, when Hitler started to gain momentum, people didn't want to see the truth back then, either. They denied it was happening. They refused to do anything against the system and it, very rapidly, took over and enslaved everybody. When people started fighting back, it was too late. Unfortunately, we're right where the system wants us to be, asleep and unprepared. So, to prepare, I tell people to store some food. Store items you can barter with later or you can protect yourself with; get some gold and silver, because if you are not totally self-sufficient you'll become a slave.

Never, in Scott's wildest dreams, had he imagined what Cook was revealing could happen in America. Mandatory inoculation for children was rumored to be part of Hilary Clinton's health plan that congress refused to pass. Could the bio-chip have secretly been in the plan? He had to know more.

The next day after making several phone calls, he managed to track down an address for Dr. Carl Sanders. That evening Scott wrote the doctor a long letter. He wondered if Sanders would understand what he was really feeling, that the hour was late for America, and that, as she slumbered, dark forces were encompassing her. The anxiety he felt was almost paralyzing. In the following days, he did a lot of praying and reading Revelation and waited, and waited for some direction.

A month later, Sander's letter was on the kitchen table when he walked in from work. Without washing up or even kissing Amy hello, he ripped open the large envelope, and collapsing on the sofa, began to read.

"Dear Scott: Thanks for your letter. I understand your concern and trust that I can answer your questions satisfactorily. Several years ago, I was involved in a research and development project as the chief engineer. I was asked to help design a micro-chip that would do a spinal by-pass on a young lady who had a severed spine. Since she was very strong, her doctors felt she was a good candidate for this experiment. We began the project in Phoenix in conjunction with the Boston Medical Center, and some people at Stanford. You may have read about it in *Readers' Digest*. We were able to give her back the use of her legs and arms.

"The by-products of that project, though, were a whole group of micro-chips. Some of these were behavior modification chips. We found that the frequency of the chip had a great affect on her, behaviorally. It would make her nauseated or very lethargic. It could do a lot of things. And so, these characteristics were saved from the project.

"As time went on, the chips became more sophisticated. And, at one point, we determined that we couldn't use a flat chip that was to be surgically implanted. We started designing stack strata, and building a cylindrical chip that could pass through the eye of a hypodermic needle.

"We spent a million and a half dollars doing research on places to fit the chip on the human body. The chip has 250,000 components. It uses a tiny internal lithium battery. We were able to build a charging circuit into it that was dependent on rapid temperature change. And the places we determined offered the greatest temperature change were just below the hair line on the forehead and on the back of the right hand.

"I fought the use of lithium as a battery source. I felt that it might cause us some problems. But I was out voted.

"Then I began to understand why, after God put a call on my life and I began studying Scripture. One day I spoke with one of the doctors at the Boston Medical Center about the use of lithium. I asked him what would happen if the chip broke down, if a blow was struck, for instance. He said it would cause a sore, a grievous sore.

"Revelation 16, verse 2, states: 'And the first went and poured out his vial upon the earth; and there fell a noisome and grievous sore upon the men which had the mark of the beast, and upon them which worshipped his image.'

"That sore is singular. They didn't break out with sores. They broke out with a sore. I believe God will erupt all those micro-chips at once.

"I am concerned, Scott, because most people have no idea what lies ahead. I feel very compelled to warn everyone. We have children in Florida right now in day care centers receiving micro-chip identification. It is being used in many, many areas. Alzheimer's patients are receiving it. The whole thing about the pictures on the milk cartons and the paper bags was government funded and was meant to condition us about lost children. It has served its purpose and you have seen it disappear. If you want to check on who paid for it, it was an organization called Evergreen, which is a C.I.A. operation.

"In closing, let me just say that God is on the throne and we win. If you'll check the tomb, it's empty. We need to be excited about that. We're living in the most exciting time in history. The

body of Christ must pull together, support one another. When I speak in meetings, people ask me,
'What shall we do? When is this going to happen?'
I tell them, the 'when' is not the big question. If
you don't know the 'who,' you're in trouble already.

Thank you, friend, for your concern. The hour,
indeed, is late. In His Name, C. Sanders."

Scott put the letter in his Bible and tried to collect
his thoughts. Sanders was convincing. But how late
was the hour? Should he follow preacher Stair's advice
and start packing? What about the fellowship? Amy
would follow his lead. Amy...

After supper was over and Amy joined him on the
sofa, he handed her Sanders's letter.

"Oh my," she said when she finished reading. "This
must mean we are much closer than we thought."

"I know."

"Do you have any direction yet?"

"That's what's driving me bonkers. Nothing. I keep
getting all this information, but for what? It was no
coincidence we were put into Lenny's cell-block. It's
no coincidence every time I turn on short-wave, someone is giving out new information that puts another
piece into the puzzle. But why? What's God telling
me? I feel I should be doing something, maybe wake
people up.

"I stopped at Pastor Carlson's last night on the way
home. He listened, but I could tell he thought I'd flip-
ped, especially when I brought up the militia. Somehow he got the idea I was telling him to arm his
church. Can you imagine that? I was just trying to
show him the extent of the unrest in the country and
how it will deeply affect every one of us.

"I didn't dare tell him about the detention camps.

He would have had a seizure on the spot. His final advice was to pat my shoulder, condescendingly, and tell me to trust the Lord, that He would take care of everything when the time came."

"No one can argue that," Amy said. "The Lord has promised He'll never desert us in time of trouble."

"I know, but that help He promised is conditional, isn't it? We've got to trust Him, to exercise faith. You can bet He'll insist on it. Most Christians in this country haven't the foggiest notion what trusting Him really means. How can they, with their insurance policies, investments, and putting pressure on their kids to get the best education to insure them of a secure future? They have no idea the control of Satan in their lives.

"They blissfully perform their religious obligations year after year, working *for* God but not *with* Him. They ignore the promptings of the Holy Spirit, making their churches social clubs with services rigidly controlled by the bulletin, instead of spiritual hospitals to nourish the battle wounds of the saints.

"So, if they haven't learned to trust Him in little things, to listen to His voice on a daily basis, what do you think they'll do when all this hits? I'll tell you what they'll do. They'll march right down to the post office with their neighbors and take that implant chip in their right hand or forehand because without it, they won't even be able to make a mortgage payment. And of course, they'll justify it by saying God would never deny them a roof over their heads and that little ID chip can't possibly be the mark of the beast."

"But not everyone is going to go along, you know. The true remnant won't."

"I know." Scott said. "But most will, to save their hides, mark my words. That reminds me, I meant to tell you. I read in the *Patriot News* that special train cars have been spotted in parts of the country with shackles built in the walls for transporting prisoners. In another case, a truck driver, curious about his load to Las Vegas, opened his crates and found shackles. The newspaper has also heard from patriots that got into some boxes on cars on a rail siding in the Cut Bank-Shelby, Montana, area and found handcuffs, shackles and guillotines."

"Guillotines?" Amy asked startled.

"That's what I said," Scott answered. He reached over for his Bible on the table. "It got me remembering something real quick. Here, listen to this. Revelation 20:4. 'And I saw thrones and they sat upon them, and judgment was given them: and I saw the souls of them that were beheaded for the witness of Jesus, and for the word of God, and which had not worshipped the beast, neither his image, neither had received his mark upon their foreheads, or in their hands; and they lived and reigned with Christ a thousand years'.

"But you know, hon, I think that soon, there's going to be a move by the New World Order crowd against born-again Christians, as well as the patriots. They don't have to wait to see who refuses the mark. We're a pain in their butt now. That's why they're building all those concentration camps. The other night I heard on short-wave there are, at least, forty converted military bases and work camps ready to go.

"There's suppose to be a camp at Allanwood Pennsylvania, one at El Reno, Oklahoma, one at Florence, Arizona, and Tule Lake, California, those are some I remember. This caller to the show had a whole list of them. He said he called the Pentagon, talked with a couple of the brass, one was provost marshal for the Fifth Army, and do you know what? These guys didn't deny that these camps were for U.S. citizens. Oh, and another interesting item, these camps are all located near interstate highways, or railroads for easy transport of large numbers of people.

"Some young guy called in the same night and said he had applied for a job at a Federal facility out west. He named the town but I couldn't get it through the static. But get this. He asked the guy interviewing him why they had such a large holding facility out in the middle of nowhere and the man answered that it was for the trouble makers in the country, the patriots and the born-again, right wing radicals."

"But they just can't start throwing people in jail, how will they do it?"

"From what I've been able to learn, here's what will probably happen. Phase one of their plan goes like this: an arrest, or perhaps a shooting provokes crowd unrest and threats against public officials and rioting starts. Phase two: some police vehicles are ambushed, maybe there's a terrorist attack against an armory, and thousands of people start to gather. Phase three: they try to disperse the crowds and arrest the most vocal before the crowd becomes sympathetic. But the local police and the National Guard can't do the job—now there's sufficient cause to turn the problem over to federal control.

"Now keep in mind, they can actually start the whole thing, themselves, whenever they think the timing is right to help their plans.

"The preparation for this is called 'Cable Splicer,' which is part of a bigger picture, 'Operation Garden Plot,' a martial law program that will give them authority to confiscate citizens' guns. Of course, the patriots will get into their face and that's when the civil war will break out."

"But peaceful people won't have to worry, right?" Amy asked hopefully.

"Come on, you know better. Remember, this whole program is designed not only to get the guns from the people, but also to stop anyone who attacks the State—even verbally. The reason patriots and Christians are targeted is because these guys know we will not submit to the New World Order. Christians won't bow to the "god of forces" and patriots won't submit to the United Nations.

"From what I've learned, their 'right-wing extremist' *hit* list includes more than born-again Christians, patriots or gun rights advocates.

"It includes all pro-life people who the government and media try to claim are guilty of a national conspiracy to firebomb abortion clinics and murder doctors.

"It includes farmers and ranchers because they don't want the government managing their lands and homesteads. It includes Internet and fax users because they are supposedly guilty of sending so-called 'hate' messages by computer and fax lines.

"And don't forget conservative talk show hosts because they provide forums where the more courageous Christians and other anti-New World Order voices talk about the outrageous acts Big Brother has committed against citizens.

"Then we've got the tax protesters, who don't understand why the IRS should exercise such massive and unconstitutional police powers over an over-taxed citizenry.

"Let's see, have I forgotten anyone? Oh, what about the Tenth Amendment people who believe that the powers not specifically given to the Federal government are reserved to the states or to the people?

"And what about our guys in the military who oppose PDD-25, that allows Clinton to turn over command of U.S. forces to United Nations commanders? Some of these military patriots put out a publication called the *The Resistor* which is causing quite a stir, even though the military brass has tried to squelch it.

And how about Michael New, that army medic with the 3rd Infantry in Germany? They told him to wear a United Nations uniform and he said, 'nothin' doin',' I took an oath to support and defend our Constitution, not the United Nations.' The Army gave him a dishonorable discharge, but he says he's taking it all the way to the Supreme Court, if he has to, because he knows he's right. They were asking him to obey an unlawful order.

"We mustn't forget people who object to homosexual conduct, they're just narrow minded and bigoted. But the fact that all nature cries out against the act because the body parts don't fit, or that reproduction is impossible and the whole human race would be wiped out if everyone practiced it, is beside the point, of course."

"Why are they so against home schooling?" Amy asked, then caught herself. "Oh I know, because there's no way to teach kids a new age, liberal curriculum if they're taught at home."

"Exactly right. So you see, anyone who doesn't fit with their agenda is labeled a 'right-wing extremist.' And the nation is being conditioned to distrust, investigate, and even quarantine these terrible people because they are a possible threat to national security."

"But these groups you've mentioned must include almost half of America," Amy insisted.

"That's about the size of it."

"And all the while the church sleeps on," Amy sighed. "What about the pastors, hon? So what if they think we're crazy, we can't give up trying to reach some of them, can we?"

"Well, Heaven knows, I've done my best to warn them. It's like talking to a wall."

"I just don't think we can ever stop trying. I know I'm not giving up, though at times, I feel like throwing my hands up in despair. Some of the women in the fellowship give each other looks when I bring up about storing food, and all. I keep praying to the Lord to open their eyes. The other day Julie said to me, 'If all this stuff you and Scott talk about is right around the corner, how come we don't hear anything about it on TV?' Can you believe it? After all we've shared, if TV or their newspaper doesn't confirm it, they refuse to believe any of it. That's how much we've all been conditioned."

Later, when they were in bed and after they had prayed together, Scott held Amy in his arms and silently thanked God that He had given him a woman who truly was supportive.

"Amy? "

"Hmmm?" she answered sleepily.

"Maybe we should think about leaving Chicago."

"I know. I've had the same thought. I've been praying that God would speak to you if He wanted us to leave."

"How about that? But where do we go? How will we support ourselves?"

"Isn't that what faith is all about, oh man of God?"

"Yeah," Scott answered sheepishly.

NINE

In the days following, Scott prayed continually about leaving the city, but he couldn't get a direction to start packing. Then one morning, while deep in prayer, he received a thought that he tried to ignore, but couldn't. It was just like when he'd gotten the inspiration for the cross at the Civic Center. The message was, *put loud speakers on your truck, go to construction sites and announce that Jesus Christ is coming soon.*

His immediate reaction was, I can't do that, I'll get busted. I'm sure to get a brick through a window. All that day, as he drove his cab around the city, it seemed every time he turned a corner, there was a new construction site he'd never noticed before.

He knew he was stuck in another "what if" situation. Several times in the past he had received a thought out of context, usually while praying, usually things hard to do like making restitution, or asking someone's forgiveness, and immediately, he would be attacked by doubt. *If you do that your wife will think less of you,* or, *your boss will fire you, etc.*

There was a way out, of course. With effort, he could just harden his heart, pretend he hadn't heard. He could lose himself in work, hobbies, perhaps, even in the Lord's work. He'd done it before, he was ashamed to admit. At first he thought he'd gotten away with something, but one day, he realized he was acting the way he used to in his old life, like noticing those tight skirts more and more. So he'd scamper back to the fold, only to find the gate to the pasture shut and not to be opened until he did what he was supposed to do in the first place.

Still, he told himself, there had to be a law somewhere that forbade loudspeakers on vehicles. One day he was passing a public library in Oak Park when his curiosity got the better of him. He went into the reference section and looked up Illinois law. Though loudspeakers were not mentioned, sound that could be heard more than 75 feet from a vehicle was illegal, and Scott surmised it was for the kids who played loud music while cruising. But it also stated: "except for advertising purposes" and this, he knew, would get him by, legally. After all, he would be advertising the Gospel.

Curious, he went to Supreme Court Cases and found in "Saia vs. N.Y." that the court had ruled that "cities may, by local ordinances, control excessive noise, and time and place (public places like parks should be left open) but cannot ban loudspeakers, or censor annoying ideas, that no local police should make persons lose time in court to prove a right already theirs."

He could procrastinate no longer.

On his next day off, he was in his black 83 Ramcharger, crowned with two new horn speakers, and headed to a large office building being erected just west of the Loop. As he approached the site, he could see men everywhere, some as high up as ten stories. He pulled into the curb with his speakers pointed right at the building, said a little prayer, took a deep breath, and pressed the mike button. A loud screeching howl about deafened him, and he sheepishly rolled up his window to eliminate the feedback. Taking another deep breath, and remembering his ham radio technique to enunciate and to keep his voice at low register, he said, "Attention, workers, attention." He paused, wondering if he was being heard over the construction noise. Some of the men had stood up and were looking his way. He pressed the button once more. "Attention, workers, attention." The men higher up were now watching him. He was getting through. His heart was pounding. He pressed the button. "Jesus Christ is coming soon. Jesus Christ is coming soon."

He wasn't ready for the reaction he received, which ranged from not a few jeers, with several vulgar fingers pointed upward, to an iron worker who held his arms out as though he were on a cross. But there was one lonely worker Scott noticed, up high and off by himself, who was waving his hard hat at him and smiling. Scott knew he had to be a believer, and that more than offset all the negative reaction from the others. But no one approached him with a sledge hammer, nor did a squad car appear.

A little more confident now, he went out again on his next day off, and a month later, received another strong impression; that next, he was to go to the restaurants and bars. Again, he balked, afraid of what might result. He turned to the Maranatha people. Though they were supportive, none volunteered to go with. Even Carmen, whom he could always count on, begged off, saying his free time was all taken up by the militia group he had joined.

Though he received many insults, Scott was only man-handled once. He was shoved out the door by a patron in a restaurant with whom he had gotten into a shouting match. After that he was careful to say only what he was sure the Lord wanted him to.

One afternoon he walked into a local pub and made his announcement. A young female bartender told him to take a hike. Three more times that week he was pressed to do the same thing and the young woman threatened to call the police. Then came the real struggle. He heard in his spirit, *go ask the girl that if she were to die tonight, would she go to Heaven?*

He couldn't believe it. This would be a major confrontation. That night he didn't sleep very well. In the morning, he called a local pastor whom he respected and had become friends with. The Bible spoke of wisdom through counsel of the brothers. "You'll never win anyone to the Lord with actions like that," was the pastor's counsel.

"Thank you," Scott sighed. "You just got me off the hook." But when he hung up, he heard, *"Will you listen to my voice or the voice of man?"* So at twelve noon the next day, he went to the bar and told the girl he had a question to ask, and when she finally calmed down, he did.

"That's it, that's it!" she cried and ran for the phone. He didn't wait for the police to show. He learned later the girl had drug problems. Two weeks after his visit the restaurant closed down.

Through the summer and fall, he visited other places with his message that Christ would soon return. He drove past baseball stands, county fairs, outdoor flea markets, even the Chicago Bears training camp in Platteville. If he heard about a parade, he would drive down the parade route 15 minutes prior to the march, speakers blaring.

Unbelievably to him, he met with little opposition—except when he visited fancy restaurants. At one, he learned an important object lesson. He had visited this particular establishment many times. He always managed to get by the hostess, walk into the center of the room, make his statement, and head for the exit, pronto.

The management began to threaten him. He pleaded with God to let him off the hook. No mater how much he prayed, nothing worked. And then, wonderfully, a verse came to him from Matthew..."if you go into a village and they don't receive you, shake the dust off and go on to the next village."

The next morning, on the way to work, he drove to the restaurant's front door, got out and stamped the dust from his feet. He said out loud, "Lord, I stand on the verse in Matthew right now because they won't receive your message." Immediately, he felt a release and never again did he have to go there. He knew then, first hand, what God thought of His word.

One Sunday he received a thought to visit a local Baptist church, and at the right moment, as when the collection was taken, to walk down the aisle and give the congregation his message. It was the hardest thing he'd been asked to do yet.

After he visited a few more churches, he had real doubt because of the lack of positive response and the oppressive spirit he felt. Many times he sat in a service, his stomach in knots, waiting for the chance to give his prophecy. He would pray, "Lord, just have the pastor ask, 'does anyone have anything to share?'" But it rarely happened because most pastors were either hopelessly caught up in tradition, or afraid of losing control. Sometimes he called a pastor in advance, but he was either turned down or told to visit the Wednesday night meeting for testimony time.

Needing encouragement, that indeed, he *was* hearing from God, he called three pastors who knew of his work with Maranatha and seemed to have finally accepted him. Not one encouraged him. They thought he was not hearing from God and was, in fact, being disruptive to the church. Doubts plagued him like never before. Still, he was being pushed to continue the message.

One Wednesday evening, he received the strong thought to visit Willowcreek, a wealthy church in Barrington, Illinois. As usual, he resisted, but then reasoned that a Wednesday night prayer meeting shouldn't be that intimidating.

But upon arriving, he found that their prayer meeting was a "community sing" consisting of about 3,000 people seated in a modern amphitheater.

"O.K., Lord, you've got to be kidding," he sighed. His first thought was to go up front and find a live mike and make his announcement just before the service. But he found none and the service began with a large choir leading the singing. When they finally left the stage, one of the pastors came out and announced he would preach from Genesis. He called the church to prayer and Scott saw his opportunity. When the pastor finished praying, Scott was standing in the center aisle, fifteen feet away, looking up at him.

"Pastor, with your permission," he began, and turning around to the audience he proclaimed loudly, "Ladies and Gentlemen, Jesus Christ sent me here tonight to tell you that He is coming soon, much sooner than anyone thinks."

At that moment, two men appeared and took him out. The audience seemed stunned. Scott expected that at least a few brave souls would have yelled "amen" impulsively, like what happened quite often in a restaurant. When he and his escorts were almost to the foyer, the pastor said over the microphone, "Satan will do anything to disrupt a service."

Scott was dumbfounded! He was being accused of being a spokesman for the evil one. His spirit was burning but he tried to maintain composure. He was friendly to the six or seven security men, with their walkie-talkies, surrounding him in the foyer; and he told them they had nothing to fear, he was leaving.

When he finally found his car, two Barrington police walked up to him.

"What's your problem?" one asked.

"Well, if you're born again, I will answer you one way, if you're not, I will answer another way," Scott addressed one of them. "Are you?"

"Yes," the officer answered.

"Okay, do you believe Jesus is coming soon?"

"Yes, I do," he said firmly.

"Then, what's wrong with me telling that to those people in there?"

"Well...you caused a disruption, they didn't like it."

"Look, I can't help that, I'm just an errand boy." He went on to tell them that he didn't just escape from Elgin State Hospital. He outlined the prophecies that had been fulfilled and when he finished, they didn't have much to say.

For the next couple of days he couldn't forget the pastor's words. He sat down and wrote him a long letter of explanation in which he stated: "...Pastor, I believe the Lord is upset with the cloistered attitude of pastors today and that's why He had me speak from your floor. Can you honestly say you would have given me five minutes to address your church if I had called you first?" (The pastor later admitted on the phone that he wouldn't have.) "But Pastor, we have a slight problem, is it possible that you over reacted to me and attributed to Satan what the Holy Spirit had ordained, therefore nullifying God's message to the people? If you agree that you spoke hastily, would you consider speaking to the people at next Wednesday's service and tell them, that though you may not agree with my methods, what I said was not wrong—that Jesus Christ is coming soon?"

It was two days later when he received a phone call from the pastor and it was obvious he had his attention. He was afraid Scott would show up at next Wednesday's service.

They got into it a bit. Scott told the man his church service wasn't Scriptural and quoted I Corin. 14:26, about how everyone should take part. The pastor's answer was that the end of the chapter says, "Let all things be done decently and in order," that Scott was not in order by speaking out. Scott was stumped for a short time till he realized Willowcreek's order wasn't New Testament order. He had not violated God's order at all. But rather than argue, he had the inspiration to say, "Pastor, I'll make a deal."

"I don't make deals," the Pastor answered.

"Here's the deal, if you'll read Mat. 10:14 to your elders, I won't be back." "And whosoever shall not receive you nor hear your words when you depart out of that house or city, shake the dust off your feet...verily I say unto you, it shall be more tolerable for Sodom and Gomorrah in the day of judgment, than for that city."

"It's a deal," the pastor said, after a long pause.

"Then I won't be back," Scott said.

Long after he had hung up the phone, Scott sat looking out the window of his tiny apartment. Amy had taken the kids shopping, and he had turned the cab in early, hoping to catch up on some rest. He had a nagging desire for a smoke and it surprised him a little, since it was almost a year now since he had quit. He began to pace, growing edgier by the moment, and finally, he made himself stop and lie down on his bed.

He knew what it was. It had been growing within him—a question that he was afraid to talk to anyone about, to Amy, even talk to God about. But he needed to know. Was he a prophet?

From his Bible study he knew that actually all Christians acted as prophets when they proclaimed the Gospel. But there was the office of prophet that most denominational churches taught had ceased after the first century. The other offices of evangelist, pastor and teacher they accepted, but not the apostle or prophet. Scott had believed it, but the more he studied, the less sure he was they were right. He didn't relish the idea of being a prophet because all those in the Bible had had a tough life and most, an ugly death.

He hated confrontation. But what he was being asked to do more and more, to come against the religious spirit that seemed to rule most denominational churches, to tear down the strongholds of tradition, to announce to a corrupt society the soon return of Jesus Christ, was becoming a burdensome chore for him.

The actual doing of it was never as stressful as the anticipation. His stomach would be in knots for days leading up to the event. Nights were spent tossing and turning until his mission was accomplished. He thought of Jonah often and how he had tried to ignore the Spirit until he found himself in the belly of a whale, and finally ended up prophesying against Nineveh. Of all the characters in the Bible, Scott understood him the best—the prophet had rebelled because of fear. His faith could not rise to the demand.

And then, something happened that changed the direction of his life. One morning he was waiting in line at the Sheraton Hotel and reading the *Tribune*. "Clinton To Attend Conference On Inner City Crisis," the article on page two began. Mayor Daley was hosting the conference that would begin the following Thursday and the President would be staying at the Hilton. Incredibly, he heard in his inner man, *take your message to the President when he walks from the hotel to the limousine*. Scott knew the police and Secret Service would be crawling all around the hotel, there was no way he would not be stopped, questioned, perhaps, even taken in and booked.

For the next two days he asked to be relieved of this distasteful act, but nothing changed, and the stress began to build, so that he was hardly able to communicate with anyone, even Amy. Especially Amy. Ever since he began prophesying, he felt that she really didn't understand what he was being called to do. The first few times he had confided in her, she was supportive as always, but when he began prophesying in a restaurant where they were having lunch, she couldn't handle the embarrassment of the stares or ugly remarks that resulted. To spare her, then, he waited till she was outside and headed toward the car, and after paying his bill, would then preach to the patrons.

The Scriptures made it clear that the prophets were never respected by their own relatives or neighbors, Jesus, himself, being the prime example. But being forewarned, did not help the hurt he felt being accused by loved ones that he was not hearing from God. The Maranatha people thought he had a lot of guts, but he felt few of them really understood his ministry. This was demonstrated to him when he put the cross up at the Civic Center. Though all were vocal in their support, a small percentage actually showed at the center.

He knew there had to be prophets in the country doing what he was. Brother Stair was one, Dave Wilkerson another, though Wilkerson's newsletters only occasionally mentioned Jesus's second coming.

A month earlier, he had seen an article in the *Chicago Tribune* about the brother who holds up the "John 3:16" sign at sporting events. Curious to know more, he wrote the columnist, asking him to pass his phone number to the man and have him call, collect. Two weeks later the brother called.

"So, tell me, brother," Scott asked him, "How many beers have you had poured down your neck?"

"I've had my moments."

"Do you get hassled by stadium officials?"

"All the time. I'm always amazed at the freedom all the other sign holders get, even some bordering on porno, but as soon as you hold up anything about the Gospel, you take a chance on getting booted."

"How'd you get the idea?"

"I was watching a basketball game being played in California on TV one night. When I saw the John 3:16 sign in the crowd, the Lord spoke to me and told me to do it in my area, the Midwest."

"You get resistance from your family or friends?"

"Some. They told me the bad things that would happen and nobody volunteered to go with. I got a Volkswagen with Jesus signs all over it, I just drive off to the game by myself, trying to be obedient."

"What does your wife think? Does she understand?"

"No," he answered hesitatingly. "I pray that some day she will."

"Well, let me encourage you, brother, my wife doesn't understand my ministry, either. But if you have the office of prophet, get prepared to be shunned and even ridiculed by those whose acceptance you would love to have—especially believers."

The night before the President's arrival, Scott paced restlessly in his tiny apartment and tried to reach down for that one extra bit of courage that would put him over the top. But the barrel was empty. After Amy went to sleep he grabbed his jacket and walked out into the cold February night, past the dark store fronts, past the snow shoveled high against the curbs, to the "drugs" sign flashing on and off down at the corner. The cashier smiled prettily at him, like always, and he bought a pack of cigarettes from her.

TEN

They were nine, three squads of three each, moving along a ridge in southern Illinois, spread out in a long line, bodies leaning against a howling cold wind. Behind them, scattered over two miles, were other nine man platoons, patterned after the effective three-man units of the Viet Cong guerrillas in Viet Nam. They were on maneuvers in a two-week intensive training program, and Carmen and Scott had been assigned to protect their platoon's rear.

Scott had finally let Carmen talk him into experiencing a militia training session. At first, it had been a welcome change, this playing soldier in the woods, from the daily drudgery to which his life seemed to have sunk. He had needed a change badly, to get away and get a new perspective, and also, to see for himself what Carmen was so high on. They had been into it for a week now, learning survival and military tactics during the day and attending lectures in the evenings.

Surprisingly, he found himself thoroughly enjoying the range shooting. He had fired large caliber rifles before, but trying to hit a silhouette at 500 yards, and beyond, with a scoped .308 was an enticing challenge. The emphasis was long distance sniper fire and he worked hard at mastering wind and elevation allowances. His instructor, a Viet Nam vet, explained that it

110

was inevitable that the real battles the militia fought in the future would be against United Nation troops who could be resisted successfully using guerrilla tactics. Scott was still convinced that killing, no matter the cause, could not be defended. But he was a sucker for a challenge and these militia guys had plenty of that for him.

They were a cross cut of America—farmers, truck drivers, teachers, lawyers, and even ministers, to Scott's surprise. They seemed to bond well, their glue, a hatred for government corruption and intrusion into the lives of private citizens, and all had a deep respect for the Constitution. They varied in age from eighteen to sixty-five, and about 10% were women. Most were gun enthusiasts, or soon to be, and whereas, most military service recruits complained continually about the food or long marches, Scott noticed these people did not.

They communicated through CB portables and each was responsible to provide his own supplies, from toilet paper to bullets. Some carried AK-47s', AR-15s', or M-16s', but most carried a family hunting rifle or shot gun, kept unloaded for safety's sake.

When the platoon stopped for a ten-minute rest, Scott and Carmen found a wind break on the sunny side of the ridge and brought out some sandwiches.

"How're your legs holdin' up?" Carmen asked.

"Much better than yesterday," Scott answered.

"Think you'll stick out the two weeks?"

"I suppose, what the heck. That cab has really turned me into blubber. I forgot what sore muscles feel like."

"Good. Even if you decide not to join us, what you'll pick up here will help when the crunch hits. Tonight John Trochmann is the speaker. He'll have the latest in troop movements around the country. Remember, he's the guy who helped start the Militia of Montana. We get all our manuals and tapes from him. There's another guy gonna speak next week on nuclear survival."

"You really think it'll come to that?"

"Listen to this guy. You're the one always quoting from Revelation. I know, most people in the church believe we get airlifted before the tribulation. Well, I plan to be prepared, just in case the Lord has different ideas."

Scott ate his sandwich and thought about it. Somehow, he wasn't sure what he really believed. He looked out across the valley, feeling the loneliness once again that had plagued him for the past couple of months, a spiritual "desert" that he suspected was caused by the withdrawal of the Spirit from his life. Rather than dwell on it, he found escape in changing his thoughts, keeping himself occupied with trivia.

"What are those guys up to?" he asked Carmen, pointing to men up ahead, digging on one side of the trail.

Carmen looked at him in an odd way. "Not for publication." He took a drink of coffee from his thermos, wiped his mouth on his sleeve, and put the stopper back in the bottle. He sat staring down at the ground for a minute or so, then looked up, and moved closer to Scott. "I guess if I can't trust you, I can't trust anybody. But beep it to yourself, okay?"

Scott was puzzled. "Sure."

"They're tunneling."

"Tunneling?"

"You see this ridge we're on? It overlooks the whole twenty mile valley. You got this ridge, you control all traffic going in or out of southern Illinois on that interstate down there. This will be the control cell of the network for this area."

"But why tunnels?"

"To connect the underground complex of supplies, hospitals and sleeping quarters, we're gonna build. The buildings of the compound will all be destroyed early in an attack. So, you go underground. Pretty clever, actually. You're protected from napalm, strafing, even the dust from nuclear fallout. One of our CO's was a tunnel rat in Nam. He spent a lot of time underground chasing the VC, so he should know. You talk about a stickler for detail. He says you dig your section 42-inches wide with a 60-inch ceiling, it better be that. Most guys are pretty careful, even though its back-breaking work, because they respect the guy. Can you imagine, for two years he climbed into those holes over there with nothing but a pistol and a flashlight?"

"I never heard any talk about Viet Cong tunnels from the vets I've talked to about that war," Scott said, taking another swig of coffee from the thermos.

"Probably, because most guys weren't involved with them, and those that were, got embarrassed by them often. Especially the guys in the 25th infantry division from Hawaii. They built their divisional headquarters at Cu Chi right on top of the Congs' most extensive tunnel system," Carmen said, laughingly. "Can you imagine, they had air conditioned offices, ice machine plants, golf courses, even swimming pools.

"At night a handful of Cong would come out of their trap doors and create havoc with directional clay-more mines and grenades, wounding guys as they slept, and it took the army a while to figure it out. One reason was the Cong would lob in mortar shells from the outside for cover.

"You got to understand, too, these tunnels were a

neat piece of work. They were started way back when they were fighting the French. They had secret escape routes and passages that zigzagged at angles of between 60 and 120 degrees to offset explosions and make a straight line of fire impossible. According to the CO, our guys would throw a gas canister into a hole, but when they went down there, they found out why it had little effect. The VC built elbows in the system that filled with water and confined the gas into a small area.

"The CO showed us how they built their trap doors. The sides of the door were beveled downwards at an angle so that it would take a lot of pressure. They were made out of vertical and horizontal boards and sponge rubber and were well camouflaged. Other smart ideas they had were ventilation and smoke shafts for cooking that ran at angles to the surface to avoid the heavy rains. They thought of everything. Many of them lived underground constantly for years.

"But the point is, it's what gave the Cong such a great advantage in that war. They had no air power, no artillery, so they redefined the ambush, the hit and run, the close-in encounter, getting so close to the enemy that they were protected from air strikes or shelling. What we've been learning is that you can beat the big guy, even if you only pin him down and continually keep him off guard, its just like winning. That's partly why the Cong beat us over there. They wore us down.

"They tell us that the Tet offensive in '68 was planned and executed in the tunnels right outside Saigon, only twenty miles away, and the success of that attack really was the turning point in the war, psychologically speaking."

It was time for the platoon to move out, so Carmen

and Scott got slowly to their feet, sore muscles refusing movement at first; but after they had walked silently together for awhile, Scott asked, "What kind of a man could live underground for years and not get demoralized?"

"A very dedicated one. The Communists were good at teaching the youth, hours each week, and they were easily convinced, while our guys only had a vague idea why they were over there. The Cong had been fighting foreigners for years, they'd seen their villages burned out with napalm, loved ones killed or tortured by a government funded by the United States. Remember, too, they were fighting on their own turf, digging into, and being supported by, the very land they loved so. They had the advantage, even without the high tech weapons.

"I don't say communism is right but I know why they beat us. They had what the people in our group here have, a willingness to die, if need be, for a cause they believe in. You should hear some of the stories of these people.

"They've had their homes seized by the IRS, their businesses bankrupted by unfair regulations, one guy had over a hundred acres of his small farm declared a "wetland" so he couldn't even make a living on it. I guess that's why I get a little impatient with Christians who don't stand up against a tyrannical government that makes its citizens victims. Well, I got news. Many of the guys I've talked to in this outfit are born-again. Now what would you say about that?"

"Amazing," Scott answered. "Especially in light of Christ's teachings about turning the other cheek and admonitions in the Bible to obey the authority we're under."

"Well, these guys know their Bible, too. They feel

the Constitution is the supreme law of the land and
that we are the government. We hired those guys in
Washington with our taxes to work for us, and when
they get corrupt, or power hungry, or whatever, we
have the right to resist their bad laws and remove them
by force, if necessary. What's right is right."

"Can't argue that," Scott answered. He hadn't heard
it put just that way before and he could see the logic,
and might even agree, that it was a valid argument for
civil disobedience—perhaps even for picking up arms.
He didn't really believe Ghandi and King would have
gotten much accomplished under Stalin or Hitler.

He was still thinking about it that evening when he
and Carmen filed into the main meeting hall of the
compound to hear John Trochmann. Trochmann was an
older guy but he walked tall as he strode to the po-
dium, trim and angular, with a no-nonsense air about
him.

"We send you greetings from Montana," Trochmann
began. "I would like to start by giving you part of a
quote given by Supreme Court Justice, Brandeis, in
1928. 'Decency, security, and liberty, alike, demand
that government officials be subject to the same rules
and conduct that are demanded of the citizens.
Government teaches its people by example. Crime is
contagious. If the government becomes a law breaker,
it breeds contempt for the law, it invites anarchy. To
declare that in the administration of criminal law the
end justifies the means, like baiting people with drugs,
would bring terrible retribution. Against that doctrine
this court should resolutely set it's face.'

"Who is our enemy?" Trochmann next asked the
audience. "Anyone who would attempt to take away
any of our rights, authored by our Creator, earned by
our forefathers, declared by our Constitution, espe-

cially, the Bill of Rights. If you keep and bear your firearms, you will bring honor to your forefathers. You will also send a very large message to the traitors in Washington.

"I must say, though, that not everyone in Washington is a lost cause. We have a number of people up there who are working closely with us on a daily basis, whose goals are the same as ours—to stop the excesses of a government that, by its actions, has declared war upon its citizens. A government which turns its tanks upon its people, for any reason, is a government with a taste for blood and a thirst for power, and must either be smartly rebuked or dreadfully feared.

"This government has given its consent to its agencies to plunder and burn our homes, ravage our property, and murder innocent citizens. This government has made the states obey rules and regulations that are contrary to their own constitutions, and the Constitution of the United States, by withholding grants or funds.

"This government has deprived us, in many cases, of benefits of trial by jury, causing tax foreclosures, and the disadvantaged to be deprived of a proper defense. This government has various bodies of armed forces, including foreign troops, and protects them in mock trials and hearings from punishment for any murders which they commit, as in the Weaver and Waco cases.

"We have a document, House Bill 3355. It refers to bringing Royal Hong Kong police into these United States to be used as Federal law enforcement. You suppose that's why government agencies are wearing ski masks more and more?

"So where do we turn when our government has betrayed us? Where did our forefathers turn? They made

117

a declaration of facts stating the abuses done to them. So have we. They prepared themselves for war with enemies, foreign and domestic. So must we. This government has rendered all the civil states defenseless by taking away their organized militia from them, and incorporating it into the National Guard or the army. And they are now in the process of disarming the unorganized militia, that's you and me, by laws that are unconstitutional, thus rendering the states susceptible to all the dangers of invasions from within and from without.

"Greater and more terrible atrocities such as those in Idaho and Waco will be committed by the present government in a desperate attempt to disarm us. We will not be disarmed. We are the militia. We're on the move. Most of the 50 states have unregulated militia units forming now. Millions of citizens are armed. Billions of rounds of high-powered ammunition have been bought just in the last year. The factories can't keep up with the demand of cartridges. We have everything we need.

"The duty of the militia, according to the Militia Act of 1792, is to oppose forces too powerful for the ordinary course of judicial proceedings, which in modern times, includes street gangs or foreign armies, corrupt police departments or corrupt BATF agents. Most judicial proceedings have become a mockery of justice.

"Our enemy has passed new laws that nullify the second amendment, and therefore, the entire Bill of Rights. For this reason local militias are now supporting sheriffs, who in a number of counties, have announced they will not enforce illegal laws. A state of rebellion exists in a number of western states and is spreading rapidly. Pentagon planners are making plans for worse case scenarios. It doesn't matter what plans they make. We are Americans. We are heavily armed. This is their worst fear. Many patriots joined the militia movement because they've had enough abuse by government employees who eat up our tax money and demand our guns. They, themselves, carry guns which we have bought for them.

"We've had enough of treason by Federal agents who shoot little boys in the back, nursing mothers in the face, and burn children alive. We don't like to hear the head of AFT, John McGraw, tell us that his outfit is prepared for more Wacos. We are prepared for government to unleash its dogs of war on us for no lawful reason. We are prepared for attempts to round us up in mass arrests and transport us to FEMA concentration camps. Government psychologists have attempted to alienate us from one another, to foster the idea of every man for himself. The militia scorns the idea of every man for himself. The militia's motto is 'all for one and one for all.'

"From now on, there will be no more Wacos. We put the government on notice. No more murder. No more plunder. No more black-clad storm troopers hiding behind ski masks. Our view of the police and sheriff is one of respect and mutual purpose. We can and will work together. The time has come when every true American must stand up and be counted. We will not give our freedom away.

"Many people still think that gun ownership has something to do with target shooting, squirrel hunting, bets competition, etc. But these can't compare to the seriousness of coming events. The real issue is not recreation. It is freedom and survival. The primary purpose for firearms is the defense of life, liberty, and property, protecting our loved ones from rape, robbery and assault, and in times of crisis, defending our nation and our kinsman from enemies, foreign and domestic. Above all, our firearms can assure our freedom. Without freedom, there is nothing—no opportunity, prosperity, no practice of our religious beliefs, no enjoyment of our culture or carrying on of heritage and tradition. You don't know what you've got until it's gone.

"'When the guns are gone, and your freedoms lie scattered at your feet, it will be far too late to say, why didn't I fight instead of sheepishly retreat, for your guns are freedom's muscle. Their strength keeps the darkness at bay. For without their known power, my friend, the darkness your liberties will slay. So when your guns are gone and your freedom lies scattered at your feet, it will be far too late to say, why didn't I fight instead of sheepishly retreat.' Mr. Watchhill said that in 1894.

"On May 30, 1992, by Executive Order, 12808, President Bush declared a national emergency to deal with a supposedly unusual and extraordinary threat to our national security. Clinton continued it for two years, in accordance with section 202D of the National Emergency Act 50USC 1622D. This allows us to be put under martial law right now. Are the Federal Republics of Yugoslavia, Sureva, and Montango a threat to us? I don't think so, but our government evidently does.

"Recently, President Clinton signed Presidential Decision Directive 25 which embraces a policy allowing subordination of United States military forces to foreign control. It is supposed to be brought before Congress for a vote. But right now they are not allowed to look at it. It's classified. In other words, we are under executive order now. Some of the Congress want to bring it back to insert several things, like allowing United States forces to challenge illegal, or militarily imprudent orders.

"Right now, as I speak, foreign troops and armament are being brought into our country, I believe, to be used against us in the future while our National Guard people are being shipped overseas for police action there. I have a newsletter called 'Taking Aim'. It states that at Fort Chaffee, Arkansas, during the first week of June, a train arrived each day, for five straight days, carrying massive amounts of UN equipment. Each of these trains were over 100 flat cars long. Actual numbers of pieces of equipment exceeded 1500.

"It is confirmed that part of the operation 'Agile Provider,' includes training for relocating civilians to concentration camps. We confirmed that a new aircraft runway, along with an internment camp, has been built near Fort Chaffee that can hold 20,000 people. This information has come from sources who work inside the fort.

"In the *Navy Times,* June of '94, an article appeared showing how the Marines are now being trained for urban warfare, crowd riot control, establishing road blocks, urban patrolling, convoy security, security check points, etc. We have taken pictures of scores of Russian chemical trucks BMP-40's being painted UN white here in the states. They are used for urban pacification. They came into Saigon as the U.S. troops left, and in minutes, each unit can take out up to 10,000 persons. We found stock piles of equipment in Hedgesville, between Billings and Great Falls, T-72 and T-80 Soviet tanks—not just used for practice shelling, or war games, as the Pentagon has said.

You ask what's an AK-47 or an M-14 to a tank or an armored personal carrier? My answer is, what's a chow

line, what's a barracks, a maintenance crew, or a foot
soldier to an AK-47 or an M-14? They can't be in their
iron hulls all the time."

As John Trochmann wound up his speech, quoting
other patriots of the past, and challenging the audience
not to let these past heroes' sacrifices be in vain, Scott
quietly left the meeting and walked out into the cool
night. A full moon lit his way and just as he decided
to walk some, he was approached from the rear.

"Wait up, man." It was Carmen.

"Sure," Scott said, and he pulled out a pack of cigarettes and offered one to his friend. They lit up and
continued down a back road leading out of the
compound.

"How'd you like him?"

"Sounds like he's done his homework."

"He's paid his dues, I'll tell you. He was a patriot
years ago when most people thought he was totally off
the wall. Then, one by one, they came around as they
saw what he'd been yelling about beginning to take
place in the country."

"He's a man pursuing a dream," Scott said, half to
himself, remembering words from his past.

"That's for sure. But what about you, ace? Convinced yet? "

"I've still got reservations. There are a lot of unanswered questions. But you know, if I decide to join
you guys, I'm in it with both feet. I just got to be sure
it's what I'm suppose to do, that's all."

"Well, if it means anything, the commander would
sure like you aboard. I told him you're a ham operator.
We need help bad with the radios. I think he'd make
you communications head, if you sign on."

"I know. You guys having to relay on CB is really
micky mouse. There are better ways. But I've been

thinking, I don't have to hurry back. My granddad had a farm south of here a long time ago, about three miles from Goreville. I spent summers with him when I was a little kid. It's deserted now. After we're done here I thought I'd check it out, maybe camp out a few days and try to put things together."

"Sounds cool," Carmen said, and the two continued along the trail, not talking any more, just enjoying the brisk night air, each absorbed in his own thoughts.

ELEVEN

The second week's training was more intense than the first, with emphasis on wilderness survival. Scott learned from the onset, that to try to survive on wild game would be folly. Stored grains were the answer, but without water even they were barely edible. Water! To his amazement, he learned that many farmers, in spite of their high yield, high tech boasting, had made no provision for electricity failures. Few had gasoline generators, or had kept their windmills working.

This evening, as he sat listening to the young instructor who had been trained in the military on chemical, biological, and nuclear warfare, and had gone through several survival courses, he was struck by the mesmerizing effect the speaker had on the audience. Most of them wrote furiously or used tape recorders. There was no talking with each other; they were there to learn how to protect their loved ones, to learn how to survive.

"We have very good reason to believe," the instructor was saying, "that if the economy collapses, or some other catastrophic event throws the country into chaos, the Soviets, thinking we are vulnerable, will execute HEMP, a high altitude, electro-magnetic pulse attack. HEMP is a 200 mile-high burst, or set of nuke

124

bursts, that will destroy every electrical device's electronic solid state circuitry within line of sight. It will not physically hurt flesh. It could come from a Soviet submarine and would take eight to ten minutes to accomplish. There will be no immediate response. The government cannot make a decision in months, much less ten minutes. Subsequently, nothing with solid-state components will work. It will get quiet, no cars running, no electricity, no phone, no communications. Maybe a '55 Ford or a windup clock will run, as will a battery-powered electronic device buried underground.

"If you see a flash anywhere, drop flat on the ground, count slowly to 200. If nothing happens, get up and head for shelter. If it's a high altitude bright flash you'll have about 15-20 minutes to get into your shelter.

"Do not mistake HEMP for a low altitude, aerial burst nuclear detonation with a big cloud, called a nudet. In the event you are in one of the safe areas, you may not see a HEMP burst. But, if suddenly the electricity goes off and you don't hear any radio stations, you can figure the attack is on. If you can't tell a HEMP burst from a low altitude burst, get to cover as fast as you can. If there is no blast and heat immediately after the flash, then you know it was a HEMP burst.

"The Soviets may use neutron warheads, called clean bombs, with little collateral damage in the ensuing nuclear lay down, to kill flesh, not crops, because they need our resources.

"Distance, mass, and time are your friends in a nuclear attack. If you're prepared, you will have a good chance of survival, if you're not too close to target cities on the east side near the target or down wind. The prevailing winds over the U.S. are west to east, fallout will be worst on the east side of any given target. If you're within 12 miles of a one megaton blast, your survival chances are slim. Soviet MIRV's are suspected to have ten, onc-megaton warheads. More damage can be caused that way than with a one, ten-megaton warhead. High winds will go out to over 25 miles in all directions. But if you're more than 25 miles west, you won't be much affected by fallout from that particular hit.

"Don't look at the fireball. You'll be blinded. However, if you're within 100-400 miles of another nudet west of you, you'll be in trouble. If you're closer than that, you'll have some chance of survival, but you'll have to have made extensive preparations and have moved fast.

"Gamma rays travel on line of sight from the nudet like rifle bullets. Alpha and Beta radiation are in the fallout, but will deteriorate within weeks. The fallout dust must be kept away from you. Get some dirt in bags, for mass, or bags of corn or wheat, second best idea, over and around your shelter. Bags can be bought at farmer's co-op for 60¢ apiece.

"If anyone goes out of the shelter, his outer clothes must be left outside the house. If possible, don't send the same person out twice. Alternate exposure, and only for short periods.

"You have to be prepared. People running around, looking for food, or looting, etc., will be dead in one to three weeks, even sooner, if closer to the nudet. Under no circumstances do you go outside during the first two or three days. Prepositioning the required items in the shelter is the ticket through this.

"Your first need will be water, at least a month's supply. You must have containers. Plastic milk jugs or

Pepsi-type two-liter jugs will be invaluable in the shelter, and later on. You're going to need at least a gallon of water a day for every person, especially, if there is vomiting. You have to flush your system of irradiated particles.

"Take two teaspoons of baking soda and four of salt, and four or five of sugar or honey in a gallon of water, during the days you are vomiting up body electrolytes, due to poisoning. Plain liquids won't do it. Gatorade will work, but it's expensive.

"Any water exposed to dust must be filtered. Other than well or spring water, all other water must be purified. Clorox will do nothing against radioactive particles. You can make a simple water filter out of a metal bucket, sand, straw, stones and dirt, or go out and purchase one now. There's 60 gallons of water in the hot water tank of most homes. Have some hose handy, and that's a swell place to build your shelter, next to the water tank.

"A hand, well pump can be installed on most wells with a fitting that allows pumping water through a hose directly to the house. You can get a local plumber to put a hand pump on your well, along with your present submersible pump. Lehman Brothers Hardware, Box 41, Kidron, Ohio 4436 (216) 857- 5441/5771. They have a catalog with hundreds of water-handling items, as well as non-electric aids.

"If you have a year-round spring, you're O.K. But, after the fallout, and the rain has cleansed the land, you'll still need clean water. You'll need Clorox or Iodine drops for spring water. One teaspoon of Clorox in ten gallons will purify, but a better purifier is food-grade Hydrogen Peroxide. Ten drops per gallon will take care of every strain of bad bacteria. But it must be food-grade. A health food store can order it for you.

"If you have a four-inch ID, or larger, well casing in your well, you can use a tubular well bucket, available for $33 from Lehman's. You drop it into the casing with a rope, the valve opens, water flows in and you have two to three gallons of water. If you're smart, you can make one out of PVC pipe, with a caged rubber ball for a valve in the bottom. You may have to pull the existing plumbing from the well casing to get your tubular well bucket down. That usually takes a three to four foot "T" handle, made out of pipe, with a $1^1/8$-inch or $1^1/4$-inch thread on the end. A plumber can make it. But see him now, forget him later.

"You can figure how much food you're going to need for at least one to four weeks, remember, you must stay in your shelter for at least one week, if you're closer to the blast, maybe four to five weeks. Pray for rain to wash away the radioactive dust.

"You must have some critical food-support items. Vitamin pills will help. Don't take aspirin, because it will hurt your tender stomach lining if you've been irradiated. Use Tylenol.

"You need Calcium Citrate, 100 mg a day, to fight off nuclear effects on bone marrow. Adults need to take five drops of Lugols Solution (potassium iodide) daily, children, two drops daily for 100 days after the fallout begins, for protection against radiation. Vitamin C, D, and B3 should be taken also.

"If possible, don't use candles or kerosene lamps in the shelter; they will use up your oxygen. Blue lips mean not enough air, fan some in somehow.

"Have flashlights and extra batteries ready. Get some boxes so you can keep everyone's stuff separate. Canned goods are great, but you must have a can opener.

"Forget about your freezer because you won't have

electricity. Dehydrated survival packages are okay, but expensive. Grains and lentils are your best bet—wheat, barley, rolled oats, beans and rice. Store them in plastic milk bottles or five gallon buckets. Get a hand grinder, now. Don't forget honey or sugar. Get boxes of powdered milk, it will keep two or three years."

As the instructor shot out his information in rapid fire order, Scott wrote non-stop. This could be critical information he would need in the future.

"Today, you can get 100 pounds of shelled corn for eight dollars at the local farmers co-op. You soak it overnight, or until it gets soft, boiling works quicker. Then put brown sugar on it. Ten pounds of dry corn will swell to about 25 pounds of food, same goes for other grain which you can buy from local farmers for $5 to $6 for 100-pounds. Same price for cow feed. In the near future it may be much higher.

"Grain or corn kernels have to be either boiled, ground or rolled—otherwise, it will go right through you. Chewing hard corn will break fillings out of your teeth.

"You'll need iodized salt, baking powder, etc. If your wife won't cooperate with you now, don't worry about it. Work alone. She'll sure cooperate with you when the bomb goes off, I guarantee it. If you can find a wholesale grocer, you can get your food stuffs in cases—makes it easier to handle.

"Wood is going to be the resource of choice for fuel. Coal keeps well, but you must use a cast iron grate in your stove to avoid ruining it. Coal will melt steel grates and stove bottoms. It also must be kept dry but it won't rot like wet wood.

"Saving old motor oil to use in starting fires is an idea, and besides, the EPA will have been blasted out of existence, anyway. You can burn it in a pinch, but be careful, it'll put out fumes, especially if you do not have an airtight stove, or your stove pipes are in poor condition.

"Heating water can be a problem unless you think ahead. You must have a lid on the water pot to heat it quickly and economically. Cast iron stuff is going to be the rage. Carbon steel knives stay sharp longer than stainless. How about a meat saw?

"You must have food-support items. What about matches or magnifying glass to start a fire?

"Buy a whole case of matches for bartering. Plumbers' candles come singly, or order them special, 200 to a box, from a hardware store. Keep them in a cool place, they melt.

"Your dollars are going to be changed into a new currency soon. Spend your dollars for these goods now. When money becomes almost useless, you'll have valuable items to barter with.

"Get a painter's dust mask (or two) for everyone in the shelter so that when you go outside you won't be breathing fallout dust. Have a bucket and plastic bags to handle human waste. If you have a basement shelter, you might cut a hole in the septic down pipe and fix something up to allow pouring urine into it; nothing else, unless you have plenty of water to flush it down. Cover each deposit in the bucket with newspaper shreds, or have a bag of lime handy.

"Toilet paper and coffee will be the rage in trade goods. Have flashlights and batteries, it's going to be dark in that shelter without them. Female necessities should not be forgotten. Keep clean with baby wipes, a box or two, for each person.

"Get yourself a short-wave radio, with plenty of extra batteries and store it in an ammo box, which you should bury before the attack. Once the nuclear atmospherics clear up, you'll be able to tell others what is happening in the rest of the world. You can get old gas mask carrier bags at a military surplus store for one dollar. They have waist and leg straps and can be used for lots of stuff, like tools, ammo, food, personal effects, etc.

"Now, here are some ideas for survival over a longer period of time. Fifty-five gallon oil drums can be obtained, usually free, from tractor service dealers, service stations, etc. You can get a 55 gallon drum-attachable rotary pump for your oil and gas from many sources, for about $70. Gasoline spoils, depending on octane rating (get 87), in a year or so, unless you treat it with 'Sta-bil,' manufactured by Gold Eagle company in Chicago. You can extend its life by about a year.

"Remember, most modern engines have solid state ignitions and will be destroyed in the HEMP attack, unless its in a root cellar, or buried, or below the line of sight of the bursts.

"A generator will be handy to run a chain saw, but do not depend on gas-powered equipment for the long haul, because gasoline won't be available. Bring any 12-volt storage batteries into the house in the winter. If they are not fully charged, they will freeze up and be worthless in the spring. There'll be none for sale during 'silent spring.'

"You'd best get some rope, tape, string, and some aluminum metal rolls and sheeting. It'll come in handy, as will silicone caulking. Lots of wire is a must. Generators and chain saws need oil, too. Think. Get extra chains for the chain saw and crosscut saws, and axes, to manually cut firewood. Get all your hand tools sharpened. Get a hack saw. A brace and bit will be useful. Go to farm auction sales and get tools cheap. Get a hand grinder from Lehman Brothers to sharpen your tools, and a whetstone to sharpen your knives.

"Now, for gardening concerns: you can get hermetically sealed seeds in cans from Walton Seeds at 1-800-847-0465. They sell for about $16 each. There are enough seeds, in foil packets, to plant a basketball court-sized garden. They'll keep for years. The Walton seeds, except for the corn, are non-hybrid. Seeds saved from matured plants this year, grown from hybrid seeds, usually will not produce much, if anything, the next year. America has trapped herself with hybrids.

"Your roto-tiller probably won't work after the HEMP attack. If it does, great. If not, you'll have to use a spade or hand plow. Fertilizer will keep forever, and in bags, can be used as mass around your shelter. Bug insecticide is another consideration. Put it in a sock and dust the plants (by tapping the sock). Canning is great, but you'll need equipment. Get it now. Buy small and wide-mouth lids. If you have extra money, get a bunch. You can barter those, too.

"As for a shelter, you can build one out of plywood in one corner of your basement if you don't have a root cellar. Second best are plastic sheets, two or three layers hung from the ceiling. Seal any basement windows and doors if time permits. Use foam spray for cracks. Any windows near the shelter should also be blocked with any solid material available. Remember, you may also have a security problem with looters who will die in a few days.

"What about sleeping? You might not have any heat, so think. If you use two by fours as studs for your shelter, you can easily make flat sleeping bunks and hang them from overhead. Cut them 24-inches by six feet.

"All this preparation might seem like a big order,

and It is. With the strong possibility of an economic collapse, you're going to have to have this kind of survival stuff, anyhow. But if you start with the most important items first—food, water, shielding, you'll live a lot longer than the folks whose first thoughts of preparation will be when they see the flash. They'll only have 20 minutes, at best. Worst case, they'll only have 20 seconds. You can be in your shelter in 20 seconds!"

That night, Scott tossed restlessly in his bunk. Nagging, fearful thoughts kept bombarding him. Part of him wanted to believe that talk of nuclear attack was ridiculous, but the sensible part cried out to take action and prepare while there was still time. The Romanian Bible smuggler's warning came back to him, "America will burn. America has become Sodom and Gomorrah in the eyes of God." His final thought before sleep eventually came was that the last place he wanted to be in case of an attack was a large city—like Chicago.

TWELVE

"So, tell me, Scott, how many countries have you worked?"

"Not that many, probably only about 100."

"I have a brother whose wife has threatened to divorce him, he's on his rig so much."

Scott laughed a little. "Yeah, I knew ham operators like that. They'd stay up all night to work a rare one."

Militia Commander Bob Dunn stood up and walked over to a brief case lying on his bunk. He was balding and lean, and could have passed as a double for Tom Landry, ex-coach of the Dallas Cowboys.

"When Carmen told me about you, I knew we should meet. Carmen says you started a church that's helped him quite a bit."

"I met him while doing street work. He was a bartender that had two loves—guns and women." They both laughed.

"Is your religion the reason you have doubts about joining us?"

"To a degree."

"We have some very, and I mean very, religious guys in this outfit. Almost every one of them had doubts about the eventual possibility of resisting their government with force. It's a tough call for a Christian, I will admit, but I think what finally convinced

134

me to get involved, beyond just putting a bumper sticker on my car, was the realization that our government is different than any other in history, especially the Roman government of Christ's day.

You and I *are* the government, every citizen in this country *is* the government. We elect representatives to go to Washington and make laws to which we all agree. If these representatives create acts of treason, or allow agencies like the ATF to be abusive, we have the right to vote then out of office and, if need be, to use force.

Our authority is the Constitution, which is supreme over the President, Congress, or the high courts. What's happened in recent years is that there have been some very corrupt people in government who made terrible decisions that hurt this country very much."

"Like Vietnam?"

"Exactly," Bob Dunn said quickly, "and way before that. But most recently, NAFTA, GATT and the Crime Bill." He had been sorting through his brief case as he spoke, and now he found a file folder, closed the case, and sat down again at his desk.

"I've never considered what government of the people really meant until recently," Scott said. "But I have to admit, armed resistance is in the Constitution."

"That's right," Bob Dunn agreed. "I cringe when I think about the implications. But then I think about my three kids and what this country will be like when they grow up, if we don't act now, and I get motivated quick". His eyes went to the folder before him. "I'll be frank, we very definitely could use your electronic skills. We've been trying to use CBs' but they're a joke. Phone lines are too vulnerable and easily tapped. We must have a dependable radio network."

"You might consider direct satellite. Trouble is,

they're not very private." Scott said.

"I know. Ever fool around with scramblers?"

"Not really."

"I played with the idea. I studied electronics in the Navy, but from what I can piece together, the government has the technology to beat us in that department. Most people have no idea the high tech advancements the government has made, particularly the Navy and its contractors.

"Take this one, for instance," Dunn referred to the folder. "It's called the High Frequency Active Auroral Research Project, or HAARP. It's a joint venture between the Air Force Geophysics Laboratory and Office of Naval Research. The project is to be constructed near Gakona, Alaska. Apparently, it's too dangerous to be built near heavily populated areas.

"By the Department of Defense's own admission, the F.A.A. was told to notify all major air carriers to avoid that corridor. They plan to saturate the atmosphere near the North Pole with one and a half billion watts. You don't need an engineer's degree to figure out that much energy has got to disrupt all radio communications over a very large portion of the earth. Even the weather has got to be affected.

"You know, as early as 1970, the Russians experimented with weather. There is considerable anecdotal evidence that the freakish weather patterns of the seventies were due to the Russian "woodpecker" transmissions you could hear on short wave constantly. The largest of their transmitters was 40 million watts. Think what one and a half billion watts might do!

"Of course, our government won't admit to it, they say their purpose is to perform geophysical probing of the ionospheric processes, or to experiment with ELF, extremely low frequency. But we found out through a good source that it will include geological tomography, which is sort of like a computerized CAT scan of the earth below ground for geological discontinuities. In other words, detection and precise location of tunnels, shelters and hardened underground structures."

Bob Dunn put the paper away and searched for another. Scott wondered if the commander knew Carmen had told him about the tunnels.

"This one I had a problem buying into," the commander said, finding another paper. "We're trying to get more info on it right now, but get this. He read, 'NASA: The Blue Beam Project deals with the religious plans of the New World Order. The project will make use of the sky as a movie screen as spaced-based laser-generating satellites project simultaneous images to the four corners of the planet, in every language, in every dialect according to region.

"'With computer animation and sound effects appearing to come from the depths of space, astonished followers of the various religions will witness their own returned Messiah in spectacularly convincing life-like realness. Then the projections of Christ, Mohammed, Budha, Xrishna, etc., will merge into one image of a man who will give an explanation of the mysteries, prophecies, and revelations of the religious books.

"'This man-image will, in fact, be the antichrist, who will explain that various Scriptures have been misunderstood, that the religions of old are responsible for turning brother against brother, nation against nation. Therefore, the world's religions must be abolished to make way for the Golden Age or the one world religion.'

"'This event will occur at a time of political anarchy, and chaos, at the edge of something big. It will result in social and religious disorder on a grand scale, including the fanatical actions of millions of pro-grammed religious fanatics, demon-possessed, to cause widespread bloodshed.'

"It goes on, but you get the gist." Bob Dunn put the paper away.

"That is mind boggling," Scott said. "I recall that Revelation thirteen says that the devil tells those dwelling on earth to make an image to the beast that was wounded, but lives on."

"Well, I'm what you call a backslidden Baptist," Bob Dunn grinned. "I don't know my Bible all that well, but that could be exactly what it's referring to." He got up and came around his desk and stuck out his hand. Scott rose to his feet and shook with him.

"I think this old world is running out of time," the commander said." Please think it over, ask the Man upstairs for an opinion. You might be surprised at the answer."

Scott smiled. "Thanks for the info. I promise you I'll give it thought and prayer. If I feel right about it, I'll give it my all."

That evening, the final of two weeks, the patriots built a large bonfire in the center of the compound, formed a large circle, prayed, and sung several songs, one of which Scott couldn't get out of his thoughts:

> Just in case you don't remember
> Let me jog your memory.
> In the church they called the Waco compound
> Back in April '93
>
> Seventeen little children
> All so helpless and so small
> Died a senseless death of gas and flames
> How many names can you recall?

138

Ron Rendleman

Seventeen little children
Doesn't it make you wonder why?
Seventeen little children
How could they deserve to die?

Maybe we should stop and ask ourselves
We've become so blind
Seventeen little children
Finally open up your mind.

How did you sleep last night, Mr. Clinton?
Tell me did you feel their pain?
Seventeen little children
Cried out and perished in the flame.

Attorney General Janet Reno
I accept your offer to resign
How can you stand for law and order?
You will answer for your crime...

The next morning, when most of the patriots drove
north out of the compound, Scott headed his Ramcharger south to a remote deserted land of his childhood.

THIRTEEN

A frigid northern wind swept down over the wooded crests, down the rocky slopes and into the bottom lands, forcing life to retreat—even the little crawling things that lived by the creek burrowed deeper into the cracks of its dried bed to escape. A hungry red tailed hawk doggedly fought the wind and scanned the creek bed with telescopic vision. Mostly, he kept to the creek, but occasionally, he made a pass to the north where a rutted road twisted into the distance, and from where the crackling sounds of someone approaching echoed through the hollows.

Scott had his truck in four wheel drive and was slowly making his way through very heavy growth of bushes and saplings. It was late in the day before he had somehow found the old gravel road that ran from the Goreville hard road to his grandfather's farm. At times, the road was only a path and without four-wheel drive, he would have given it up.

When he finally pulled into the quarter mile driveway that led up the hill to the old farmhouse, the saplings were too large to bulldoze through. He got out, grabbed his camping gear, sleeping bag, and a .223 Ruger Mini-14 that Carmen loaned him, and trudged up the hill.

The wind was raw. He would build a fire and if he really got cold, he would sleep in the Ramcharger. He had taken out the rear bench seat before he left, just in case.

The house barely stood, deserted for too many years, a sad testament for Scott. He remembered romping through it with his cousins as a happy youngster; he remembered Grandma Nellie's hot biscuits and gravy in the cool mornings, and the supper of fried chicken on the back screened porch on a warm summers evenings.

He walked into a doorless front room and almost fell through the floor when he stepped on a rotted board. He backed out carefully, not wanting to linger in the depressing ruins littered with debris. He pried some floor boards out of the front porch, built a fire in the front yard, and poured himself coffee from the thermos.

He sat back against his gear and remembered how he felt when he had learned from his mother that the farm, along with dozens of others on the ridge, had been sold. The TVA flooded 18 miles of bottom land to form Lake Egypt and the reservoir they needed for their power plant.

He wondered how she could be so matter-of-fact about it, until he remembered her childhood on the farm had not been a happy one. Still, every summer she had sent him "down home," to get him away from the influence of the city for awhile. At first, he had been fearful as a little guy, but he soon learned that grandpa's bark had no bite, that Grandma Nellie, though so tall and sometimes stern, had a lot of love.

Many summer nights he would sit with her in the front yard and rub her swollen ankles and watch the bats swoop, and listen to her stories. And they were wonderful stories of olden times, of her childhood adventures with the Cherokees, and the things they had taught her about herbs and snakes and making arrowheads, and she would tell him how she had acquired each relic taken out of her rawhide bag.

Scott built up the fire and unrolled his sleeping bag. The wind had slackened and the sky was clear and now as it grew dark, he lay on his back, awed by the majestic scene above. No pollution here, no clouds, just millions of shimmering gems, the obvious handiwork of a Master Crafter, and he knew that the reason Grandma Nellie had come through her hard life without bitterness, and had a quality of love he envied, was because she loved God.

He stayed at the farm site the better part of a week, shooting and clumsily skinning a rabbit and two squirrels, trying to put into practice what he'd learned in the survival course. Luckily, the water from the well at the side of the house was as fresh and cold as he had remembered. He went for hikes, trying to find a tree or a pond from the past, but nature and the years had had their way.

One afternoon he walked down to the bottom land where corn once grew thick and tall, but had now become a lake. It had warmed considerably so he swam for awhile, and afterwards, he lay on his back in the tall grass on the bank and let the sun bore into him. And as he lay there, relaxed and peaceful, it seemed with each deep breath, strength flowed into him that gave him a confidence to speak out loud, "Lord, I've been away a long time. Once you asked me to do a hard thing, to witness to the President, but I wasn't willing to trust you to take me through it. Just give me another chance. I won't screw up next time."

He lay listening then, to crickets and the gibbering

of a red-winged blackbird in the nearby grass that thought him too close to her nest. Just before he fell asleep he made a final request. "Lord, I'm scared about the future, real scared. What should I do?"

His trip back to Chicago was uneventful; except, he found himself returning to his old habit of announcing at truck stops along the way of Christ's soon return. On the whole, reaction was polite. Once a trucker in back yelled "amen" at him and he knew it wasn't a dig.

When he hit the front door, Amy gave him a big hug and kiss. When he told her everything that had happened, especially the day by the lake, she beamed, and when he finally finished, she asked, "How soon do we pack?"

Surprised, he asked, "To go where?"

"To southern Illinois, of course. Don't you see, it's perfect. We could rent an old farmhouse and live off a garden, get some chickens, I think I can still remember what Mom taught me about canning."

"And the kids?"

"We can home school them. We've always talked about it, now's our chance. You would not believe what the women in the body say their kids are being taught in the lower grades. They're talking about giving condoms to all the eighth-graders."

"That's nuts." Scott said disgustingly.

"Where will it end?" Amy sighed.

"I wonder how long it will take before they start teaching homosexuality to these kids?" Scott asked.

Amy stood and went to her Bible lying on a table. Opening it, she took out a folded up newspaper page. "I brought this home from the meeting the other night. Clarice gave it to me; her sister sent it to her from Boston."

Scott opened the paper and found a ¼ page ad from

the *Boston Daily*. It read:

"Homosexuals to Parents: We shall sodomize your sons, emblems of your feeble masculinity, of your shallow dreams and vulgarities. We shall seduce them in your schools, in your dormitories, in your gymnasiums, in your locker rooms, in your sports arenas, in your seminaries, in your truck stops, in your all-male clubs, in your houses of congress: wherever men are together, your sons shall become our minions and do our bidding. They will be recast in our image.

"They will come to praise and adore us. All laws banning homosexuality activity will be revoked. If you dare cry fagot, fairy, queer, at us, we will stab you in your cowardly heart. All churches that condemn us will be closed. Our only gods are handsome young men. We shall be victorious because we are filled with the ferocious bitterness of the oppressed. We, too, are capable of firing guns and manning the barricades of ultimate revolution. Signed–Boston's Gay Community."

Scott couldn't believe it. How could a respected newspaper even consider accepting such an ad? "What's happening to this country?" he asked Amy. "It makes me sick. The liberals of the media try to brainwash us into giving homosexuals uncensored freedom, but this ad proves what I've been saying all along—these guys don't just want equal rights, they have an agenda. They are far more militant than they let on and they want our kids!" He held his head in both hands. "Man, it makes me sick to my stomach. How it must grieve God."

That night when Scott knelt with Amy to pray, he prayed that God would tell them when to leave Chicago.

He returned to his cab driving, so as not to dip into the little they had saved up, and waited for a definite leading. But as the winter weeks wore on, no leading came. What did happen was, the Maranatha meetings became more exciting, with physical healings and personal re-dedications occurring regularly, and the bond between them all greatly strengthened.

"Scott's feeling of impending tribulation, and that Christians should make preparation, never left him. But now, to his amazement, his people urged him to teach them about survival. When the truth hit him, that the Holy Spirit was, at last, confirming his warning to the Maranatha people, he poured himself into his lessons, making doubly sure to emphasize that "the just shall walk by faith, not by sight," that though it might wake Christians with a jolt from lethargy, they must not make fear their constant companion, for its only goal was to destroy their faith.

And the Maranatha people quietly went about the business of stockpiling.

Amy was as excited as he about the change in the meetings and now talked less of leaving. For a long time, they had both felt that many would leave with them when the time came, and they discussed setting up a commune. But gradually, as many in the group expressed concern about leaving family members behind, they all agreed, God seemed to be leading them to stay together to minister spiritually and physically to their community when hard times hit.

Chicago's winter was somewhat mild compared to some Scott had known, but he was still happy when

April 1st finally came, for he hoped to plant his first garden in the vacant lot next door. But it rained much the first two weeks of April, so he put off buying any seeds. On April 19th he parked his cab in front of a hardware store on Broadway and went in and bought his seeds. He was at the checkout counter when an announcer on the TV set above the counter reported that the Murrah Building in Oklahoma City had been bombed.

FOURTEEN

He listened to the news all day in his cab and that night, while Amy stayed glued to the TV, he monitored his short-wave for more accurate information. He learned someone had parked a vehicle in front of the Murrah Federal Building and virtually destroyed it with a bomb the authorities claimed was fertilizer and fuel oil, killing and injuring hundreds.

At first, spokesmen hinted that Moslem Fundamentalists were responsible, but then suggested that because the bombing occurred on the anniversary of the Branch Davidian siege at Waco, a U.S. terrorist could have caused it.

In his heart, he hoped a patriot group was not responsible because it would set back their cause by years and turn mainstream America against them. Two days later, Timothy McVeigh, 27, who had been sitting in jail on a traffic violation, was charged with the crime.

Scott's family was sitting at supper and watching Tom Brokaw when they first learned that McVeigh was claimed to have ties with the militia of Michigan, a "radical anti-government paramilitary group" as the announcer put it, and went on to explain that such groups were in at least 26 states and growing rapidly.

"I smell something," Scott said, finishing his meal

and getting up.

"What, honey?"

"Alright, let me ask you. If you were smart enough to plan out this bombing, would you then go speeding down an interstate in an unlicensed car. And knowing that you had killed many people, would you then not shoot the officer who stops you? They say McVeigh was carrying a gun. Give me a break."

Amy looked at him quizzically. "You know, I never thought of it."

"Probably most people won't. I think the reason I did it is that I'm suspicious of anything I hear these days."

Scott spent the remaining hours of the evening and the rest of the week listening to Mark Koernke, Eric and Robby of Viking International, Tom Valentine, and Bill Cooper. Koernke and Cooper were the first to suggest the government might be behind the bombing. Initially, Scott found the concept incredible, but as the days went by, more questions began to surface that government spokesmen were not addressing.

True to his fears, the media portrayed the militias as extremists or "wackos." When they interviewed a militia leader, they would edit his statements. Bo Gritz, patriot and Viet Nam war hero, was shown giving a speech and saying, "this bombing is a Rembrandt" and they cut out the rest of his remarks in which he was trying to show that only a skilled demolition expert would have known how to cause such a blast.

Scott watched one network news show try to marry the patriot movement to the American Nazis and Ku Klux Klan. The one show he felt had even been half-way fair was Ted Koppel's "Town Meeting," shot live at Dexter, Michigan, in which, townspeople aired their concerns, whether it was about the government or the

148

Michigan militia. But most of the media were anti-militia, anti-patriot, and the conspiracy theory seemed more believable to him than ever.

The President's inflammatory rhetoric was intimidating as he accused talk shows of spreading hate, promised to increase the number of police, and give the FBI broader powers of intrusion into private lives. He was "showboating," Scott surmised, because any thinking person knew that none of these measures would stop a determined terrorist with the element of surprise.

Meanwhile, interesting intelligence continued coming in on his short-wave. The night before Mark Koernke was taken off WWCR due to FCC pressure, Scott surmised, Mark and his co-host, John Statmiller, talked with Ted Gunderson, retired from the FBI after 29 years. Gunderson had conducted his own investigation, starting with the theory of two bomb blasts, and confirmed with Dr. Ken Luza, of Oklahoma University, that two distinct surface waves had appeared on their seismograph, ten seconds apart. The government said there had been only one explosion.

Gunderson said, after conferring with his explosion experts, that a low frequency fertilizer bomb could not have caused the damage the federal building underwent. He suggested that the actual bomb used was an electrohydro dynamic gaseous fuel device known as a barometric bomb, similar to the Army's 282 bomb called a daisy cutter, very small, very destructive. One of Gunderson's experts had actually helped invent this bomb.

"If I were on the other side and setting this thing up," Gunderson told his hosts, "I would get a couple of guys out of Kansas, send them to a militia meeting or two, let them experiment, or have them hobnob with people who experimented with bombs. I would have them write letters to a newspaper, complaining about the government, just as McVeigh did to an editor in New York. I would have them rent a truck to get attention, register at a nearby motel using their own names, and make sure they were seen around the courthouse, etc. No, there are too many questions about this entire affair that need answering. But let me make it clear. There are many fine, honest people working in the FBI who are just as appalled at this atrocity as the patriots are."

Gunderson concluded by revealing he had offered *Hard Copy* an exclusive on his story, but was ignored. On the same show, Mark Koernke brought out how unprofessional the FBI was in handling McVeigh. He was quite visible in a bright orange jumpsuit as they walked him over 100 feet to a van that should have been parked up against the building, almost as if they were uncaring in exposing him to danger.

Another night, Scott learned from his radio that the DEA and ATF offices were empty the morning of the blast, that undetonated charges had been found by rescuers who were stopped in their critical work of saving lives, as government people removed the materials from the building.

He learned, too, that a retired General Ben Partin, who had extensive military experience with explosives, did a very detailed examination of the building and concluded that it had been brought down by charges attached to each column. The general's analytical report to all the senators and congressmen went unanswered.

And why, he wondered, was the building removed so soon after the bombing, trucked out to a landfill, and fenced off as a restricted area? Many believed it was done to conceal evidence that the column bombs had been used. The government's reason for the quick action—there was a dead body in the debris and they didn't want to "desecrate the dead." What continued to be bothersome, too, was that while the mainstream media somehow had become deaf and dumb, the patriot talk shows and publications were pursuing these issues with tenacity.

Late one night about a week later, Scott was awakened by a phone call.

"Hi, it's me." Carmen said. "Sorry to call so late, but I wanted you to hear it from me so you'll have the straight poop."

"What are you talking about?"

"I'm leaving. I got a call tonight from my people. They want me down there. The ATF tried to force an entry on our guys and they resisted."

"You're kidding. What are they after?"

"Fertilizer, you know, stuff for a bomb. They claimed they got an anonymous tip. It's just so much bull. We don't have that stuff. Clinton wants a test case, well, he got one."

"Wait a minute. Why not give them access, let them poke around."

"Come on, Dunn would never okay that. He knows the government's agenda, it's just an excuse. The only legal authority he'll recognize is the county sheriff, but the sheriff ain't playing their game either, because he knows his authority under the Constitution. Besides, we got the tunnels, remember? "They don't need to know about them, yet."

"So what's your plan?"

"To get down there, pronto. I guess the entire unit was contacted."

"Won't they stop you before you get inside?"

"Not if I get down there tonight. They haven't even tried to close the perimeters yet, too much area to cover. Remember when we were on maneuvers, I showed you two different access routes back in those woods that you practically had to stumble on to find? Well, there are two other ways that go right into the tunnels that I didn't show you. But listen, I need you to pray. I know God listens to you. I admit I'm scared. We talked big about taking a stand, we knew it was coming, now it's time. You feel like taking a little drive?" he laughed nervously. Scott didn't answer.

"Hey, I know how you feel, you got your orders, I got mine. Just do me one favor. You've got my word we have nothing down there even close to a bomb. If something screws up, get a hold of Walter Jacobsen at Fox News, he'll at least listen. But get the truth out, some way, somehow."

"You know I'll do all I can. But listen, you don't have to go down there..."

"I'm running behind, I better go. Just pray for me. Pray hard." And he hung up.

Amy was still asleep beside him in bed. Very quietly he slipped to his knees and began to pray. And as he prayed the anguishing prayer of intercession, he began to weep for his friend.

The next morning, instead of driving north to work, he turned the Ramcharger south, down the Outer Drive along the lakefront to Navy Pier. He pulled into the vacant parking lot of Rocky's Fish House, not yet open for the season, and sat and watched the seagulls dive into the lake's waves, sparkling from the bright morning sun. This was his favorite spot in all Chicago.

Through the years he had come here whenever be needed to escape. In the summer, international trade ships that had sailed into the Great Lakes through the

St. Lawrence Seaway docked at Navy Pier. And in the summer, one could sit and watch yachts and tourist cruise boats make their way in and out of the locks of the Chicago River. But no one served fish chips like Rocky. When aged Rocky finally passed away, Scott missed his stories of fishing on Lake Michigan in the old days.

He was tuned to WGN on the radio and was listening to Bob Collins chat about his Harley, when at the 7:30 a.m. newsbreak the first report came through. The FBI and ATF had tried to enter a right wing militia headquarters in southern Illinois near Fergestown, north of Marion. They were acting on a tip that the militia had bombs similar to the one used in Oklahoma City. The agencies were refused entry and were now in the process of bringing in additional personnel and equipment.

Scott sat reflecting on the report. There were a hundred and fifty or so militia in Carmen's unit and many were veterans with combat experience. If the Feds blasted or burned down the compound's buildings, the resisters would go into their tunnels so that the conflict would be lengthened, increasing casualties on both sides. Sadness crept through him as he realized that this stand by the patriots might escalate into a civil war that could sweep across the country. Regardless of the right or wrong of it, he was sure there would be much suffering. America, the land of the free, would become the land of sorrows.

He thought to plead with God to intercede even as he knew that God had every right to be hard of hearing. Americans had been hard of hearing of the things that mattered to God for a long time.

Still, he felt increasingly pressed that he could not just sit and do nothing. He felt guilt for not having gone with Carmen. He really did believe in the patriot cause but he still couldn't come to terms with their methods. What kept occurring to him was that he was a citizen of Heaven first, and of America second. The return of Christ had to be only a handful of years away. To sacrifice everything to try to save a self-destructing homeland, while a greater kingdom's work was ignored seemed illogical, especially if one had the calling of a prophet.

For a long time he sat and pondered it. He never did get to work that day, and later at supper, said very little. After supper he put his little son and daughter on his knees and played "pony" with them longer than usual, and then, lovingly carried them into the bedroom and put them to bed.

"That was sweet, dear," Amy said when he walked into the room. "It means so much to them, you know."

"I know," he said quietly. "Would you make some sandwiches, maybe six or so."

" Oh? "

"I've decided to go to southern Illinois. I'm leaving as soon as I get everything packed."

"To where Carmen is?"

"Yes."

"Oh, Scott, why?"

"I've got to go, please don't make it any harder."

Amy turned to the sink where she had been washing the dishes and held onto it for support. Scott went out and down the stairs and began packing the Ramcharger with his sleeping bag and camping gear, and when he had everything together, he went back into the garage and made sure he hadn't forgotten anything. Upstairs, a tall angular woman still stood in front of her sink half full of dishes and wept, certain that she would never see her man alive again.

FIFTEEN

Johnny Zoe drove along the frontage road of Interstate 57 in his 1974 black Corvette, his attention focused on a timber ridge high up to his right and parallel with the road. As always, he drove with the top down; he was deeply tanned with short cropped sandy hair just beginning to recede, and he wore Avanti polarized sunglasses that really helped with the glare and gave him a youthful look. He wasn't very big, just under five foot eight, but he was trim; he was in better shape than most guys he knew because his profession demanded it. He worked for the Bureau of Alcohol, Tobacco and Firearms, and his specialty was long distance shooting. Up ahead on that ridge somewhere was his assignment.

Just behind his seat, lay his favorite rifle in its aluminum case, a Remington 700 VS .308 bolt action that weighed nine pounds, had a free floating 26-inch barrel, and a textured black Kevlar composition stock with an aluminum bedding block that ran the full length of the receiver. The bureau had recently ordered a half dozen .50 caliber sniper rifles, big heavy brutes, but he wasn't interested. With his 6.5 x 20 variable scope, he could put a 168 grain bullet, that normally dropped 50 inches at 500 yards, into a 10-inch pattern at twice that distance.

He had been with the bureau nine years.

After awhile he came to the first checkpoint. He flashed his ID, and driving on, began to pass various government vehicles and satellite dish vans of the media parked on both sides of the road. When he found the designated command vehicle, he parked, got out, and stretching his lower back, looked up at the ridge.

High up at the edge of the timber line was a large farmhouse surrounded by several smaller frame buildings. He could see why the bureau had pulled hack to the road after being refused entry; the long sloping hill offered little protection. A large steel padlocked gate now blocked the other end of the lane to the compound.

He estimated there were perhaps two hundred men sitting in various vehicles, or standing around talking. Most were dressed in black fatigues.

Taking his case and overnight gear, he walked up to the command vehicle.

"John Zoe checking in," he said to the balding desk-type staffer sitting at the card table next to the command car.

"Zoe, lets see, yes, from St. Louis. Got you down. Sleeping tent and chow wagon are down at the other end. Pre-mission briefing is at six tonight."

"Right," Zoe answered, and he took the two-way radio handed him.

He walked down the long row of vehicles, looking for a familiar face. He could use a cold beer but he doubted if there would be any around. Most of the people were from Chicago and not familiar to him. He stopped at a group of five or six younger ATF agents hanging around a pickup. He accepted a Pepsi from the one doing all the talking.

"The way I see it," the agent was saying, "those

people at Waco had every chance in the world, hell, we gave then 51 days, didn't we?"

"I still say it would have been better for everyone if you guys had just picked Koresh up in town," a second agent answered.

"Well, hindsight is always better you know, but it wasn't my decision, even our COs' were out of the planning early on. When we turned it over to the FBI, all the heat fell on them. Hell, even their own behavioral experts tried to warn them they weren't dealing with a hostage situation. This was a cult.

"What about those guys up there?" The second agent asked, gesturing to the ridge above.

"This is different. The way I see it, this will go down very quick and clean. These weekend marauders sound dedicated, but when they get pushed hard they'll give up, most of them are older guys with families. Why do you think the chief isn't keeping the press two and a half miles back like we did at Waco? You watch. Harding will be operating strictly by the book, and he'll have a great example for the rest of the country of what will happen to these militia guys when they buck heads with the government."

There was general agreement from the others, including Zoe. Anyone knew you didn't resist a law officer. You submitted to him, regardless of the circumstances—later on, you were entitled to due process. The law was supreme, especially the Federal government's.

At six o'clock he was sitting on a hillside toward the rear of a group of ATF and FBI agents who pretty much sat with their own clans, smoking, chatting, and occasionally, laughing out loud. They were mostly young men, inexperienced for this type of assault, whose "pack" mentality didn't allow the questioning of moral issues. Their motto might easily have been, "we do not think, we obey."

When John Harding stood up, the group quieted. He was middle-aged, wore black fatigues, and had eyes that darted back and forth quickly as he addressed the men.

"I'm John Harding, for those of you who may not know, special agent in charge of FBI field operations. What we have here is an undetermined number of armed civilians who call themselves "The Watchmen" and have refused our request to search the premises. On Friday of last week, we received an anonymous phone call in Chicago that these people have a large amount of ammonia nitrate and a number of illegal automatic weapons. We also have information that two individuals in the group have had contact with McVeigh, charged with the Oklahoma City bombing, on several occasions in the past. Admittedly, our probable cause could be stronger, but Washington makes the call, and the call is, that we make dynamic entry early as possible.

"We've allowed the media access. Don't be concerned, just do your job. Washington wants the country to see a well-executed operation against extremists who refuse to obey the law. Both agencies will share equally in the operation to demonstrate to the country that the two bureaus can work effectively together.

"We commence at sunrise tomorrow, approximately 0520, but be in your assigned positions by 0400. We will give them one more chance to comply, hold off for fifteen minutes, then move in from three sides. You will all carry shields. The approach directly up the front lane will be the least protected, and that's where I want Zoe and our two guys providing long distance cover. Once we give the green light to engage, anything that moves is to be taken out. You three establish your approximate positions while there's still light today, but don't be obvious.

"We'll be using automatic rifles only, we don't want to appear heavy-handed, For the same reason, we have opted to hold back the Blackhawks and the Bradley. Any questions so far?"

An agent in the front raised his hand. "Sir, what if they use explosives?"

"We pull back immediately to a safe position, but that, gentlemen, is what we are hoping for."

Some of the men looked at each other.

"It gives us the excuse to use heavy ordnance. If they continue to resist, we are prepared to level the place."

There were more questions to do with details and then the meeting adjourned.

Johnny Zoe found the two FBI shooters making their way to the base of the hill. "Not a lot of cover," he said to them, looking up to the ridge. They agreed.

There were a half dozen trees, a gully or two, some tall grass near the road they walked on. They selected their positions and Zoe opted for one of the gullies about a third of the way up the hill. He estimated the distance to the nearest building from the gully to be between five and six hundred yards. Not too tricky, if the wind cooperated.

Always the wind. One needed to know the wind, how to read the moving leaves and grass at mid range, it was referred to as reading the mirage. He saw himself lying prone in the gully, searching the buildings with the light gathering scope in the gray of early light. He saw the imagined target in a window and as he zeroed in, concentrated on his bio-feedback, fighting the adrenaline rush, slowing down his breathing, actually willing his heartbeat to fall to 40 beats; and then taking a final deep breath, and holding half of the next, he would count one thousand one, one thousand two, and if he couldn't get the shot off by six thousand, he would abort and begin again. Such was the patience of a sniper, the supreme predator, and he neither gloried in it nor despised the killing part. It was a job, a decent living.

Before he joined the government he had freelanced some, and one time for four days, lay in a Columbian swamp, stalking a political bigwig who opposed the CIA's dictates. He knew how to obey orders, and because he always got the job done, he was respected and that went a long way.

He checked out his equipment before retiring around 11:00 and slept soundly for four hours. At 3:45 the next morning, he was in his position in the gully, lying on a poncho and taking readings from his range finder scope. The distance to a lit upper window of the farmhouse was 522 yards.

At 0525 hours exactly, a loudspeaker on the roof of a government vehicle behind him on the road blasted, "Attention, attention. This is the FBI and ATF. We have a court order to enter your premises to do an inspection. Will you cooperate?"

Harding addressed the compound three times and then it was extraordinarily quiet. Zoe searched the buildings with his scope. He could see people inside darting quickly past the windows. The sun was just coming up.

"Zoe, you read?" his portable radio asked.

"Zoe here." he answered.

"Zoe, this is Harding. What can you see?"

"A lot of movement, Sir. I see weapons beginning to appear in the windows now."

"Alright. Get ready. I'll give the order over the loud speaker. Remember, take out anything that moves. Keep their heads down."

"Yes sir."

He lay the radio beside him on the poncho, pulled back the rifle's bolt to engage the first round into the chamber, and began to breath deeply. The sky behind the compound was now a deep, vivid red. Slowly, he scanned the buildings for his first target.

And then, appearing out of the shadows, a man moved quickly across the compound's open yard, carrying something large. Zoe wasn't sure of the object, nor did he really care. He was tracking the target, the man, and just as he put the scope's crosshairs on the man's head, the loudspeaker behind him announced, "We have a green light, I repeat, we have a green light."

Amy had just tucked the kids in and poured herself a cup of coffee. She walked over to the kitchen counter and turned the TV on. Peter Jennings was saying how the militia had just been given a last warning, when the camera zoomed to inside the compound and to a man silhouetted against a brilliant sky, holding a large cross. And then, Amy and the country watched in horror as the back of Scott's head blew apart, splattering the cross he held with his blood.

End

ACKNOWLEDGMENTS

The author wishes to thank the following persons and organizations for broadcasting or publishing certain critical information included in this book.

Jack McLamb   *(Vampire Killer 2000)*
Bill Cooper   *(Behold A Pale Horse)*
Terry Cook
Brother Stair   (Overcomer Broadcast)
Brother Ben   *(70th Week Magazine)*
Texe Marrs
John Trochmann   (Militia of Montana)
Mark Koernke
George Eaton   *(Patriot Report)*
James Lloyd   *(Christian Media)*
Tom Valentine
The Spotlight
Linda Thompson
Dr. Rod Lewis
Lou Epton
Larry Bates
Dr. Norm Resnick   (USA Patriot Network)
Viking Trading Int.
Dr. Carl Sanders
Forbidden Sciences
Carl Klang   ("17 Little Children")
Jim Jaret   (US Marksmanship Acad.)
Demitru Dudaman   *(Through The Fire)*

Where you moved by Scott's story? Do you agree that its information should be widely circulated as soon as possible? Why not order additional copies for those persons special to you? Just fill their names in below.

If your local bookstore cannot supply you, you may send $9.95 + $3.00 (shipping and handling for each book, Illinois residents add 62¢ tax) to:

STERLING PRODUCTIONS
P.O. Box 41
Sterling, IL 61081

(Cash, check or money order only)

- - - - - - - - - - - - - - - - - - -

PLEASE PRINT

Name _____

Street _____

City _____ St _____ Zip _____

- - - - - - - - - - - - - - - - - - -

Name _____

Street _____

City _____ St _____ Zip _____

- - - - - - - - - - - - - - - - - - -

☐ Please send me information on other books by Ron Rendleman when they are released.

Name _____

Street _____

City _____ St _____ Zip _____